"I want to see you again."

Reed stepped closer, and Antonia could feel, as well as smell, the heat of his body. "Now, don't give me any nonsense about its not being a good idea or 'What will Celia say,'" he added huskily. "Just say yes, for once in your life, without weighing the pros and cons."

"I can't…"

"Oh, for Pete's sake!"

"I can't," she repeated unsteadily, stepping back from him. With the warmth and the musky male scent of him enveloping her, it was incredibly difficult to refuse him, but the sanity of reason eventually prevailed.

"Look," Antonia said stiffly, "I have no intention of providing a novelty for you or anyone else, and if you want a *gutter* experience, I suggest you look elsewhere!"

Books by Anne Mather

STORMSPELL
WILD CONCERTO
HIDDEN IN THE FLAME

HARLEQUIN PRESENTS

HARLEQUIN ROMANCE

These books may be available at your local bookseller.

Don't miss any of our special offers. Write to us at the following address for information on our newest releases.

Harlequin Reader Service
P.O. Box 52040, Phoenix, AZ 85072-2040
Canadian address: P.O. Box 2800, Postal Station A,
5170 Yonge St., Willowdale, Ont. M2N 6J3

ANNE MATHER

act of possession

Harlequin Books

TORONTO • NEW YORK • LONDON
AMSTERDAM • PARIS • SYDNEY • HAMBURG
STOCKHOLM • ATHENS • TOKYO • MILAN

Harlequin Presents first edition August 1985
ISBN 0-373-10810-9

Original hardcover edition published in 1985
by Mills & Boon Limited

CHAPTER ONE

'Do come! It's just going to be an informal affair,' invited Celia warmly, her friendly smile brightening the rather gloomy hallway of the apartment building. 'I'm sure it's not much fun, living next door to someone who's constantly giving parties!' She grimaced. 'That's Liz's fault really; but this time I'm to blame. It's just a little celebration, you see, for a few friends. A kind of delayed birthday-cum-engagement party combined!'

Antonia's eyes widened. 'You're engaged!' she exclaimed, looking swiftly at Celia's bare finger, and the other girl laughed.

'I shall be after tomorrow evening,' she confessed, with a contented sigh. 'I'm going to marry Reed Gallagher. You may have seen his car outside. He drives a super black Lamborghini!'

'Oh, yes.' Antonia smiled. 'I think I know the one you mean.'

'How could you miss it?' exclaimed Celia dramatically. 'Well? Will you come? I wish you would.'

Antonia hesitated. Since moving into the ground floor apartment of the converted Victorian mansion six weeks ago, she had had little opportunity to get to know her neighbours. Her work at the institute kept her pretty much occupied, and besides, she had not come to London to enjoy a social life.

Nevertheless, she had not been able to ignore the occupants of the apartment above her own. They were the kind of people she had hitherto only read about in glossy magazines, their lifestyle totally different from her own. According to Mrs Francis—who was the caretaker's wife and inclined to gossip—Celia Lytton-Smythe was the only daughter of the Conservative member of parliament for one of the south London constituencies, while her flatmate Liz, *Elizabeth* Ashford actually, was very well-connected.

Whatever the truth of it, and Antonia had no reason to doubt what Mrs Francis had said, they seemed nice girls. In fact, Antonia had only spoken to Celia, but she was not opposed to being friendly with both of them. Even so, she had no wish to get involved in a situation where she was obliged to return their hospitality. The salary she was getting at the institute was useful, but she did not fool herself that things were going to be easy. The rent for the apartment, for example, was still quite considerable, even if Uncle Harry had reduced the burden, and she wanted to be able to send some money home to her mother for Susie. Giving extravagant parties was simply beyond her means. Perhaps it would be more honest to admit that right away.

'It's very kind of you, Celia,' she murmured now, shifting the carrier bag containing her week's shopping from one hand to the other, 'but I really don't think——'

'Oh, don't say no!' Celia tilted her head disarmingly, the inverted bell of her hair swinging confidingly against her cheek. 'I'm sure it can't be much fun, sitting down here on your own every night.' She dimpled ruefully. 'Forgive me, if that sounds impertinent, but both Liz and I have noticed, you don't get many visitors.'

Antonia coloured. She couldn't help it. Even though she surmised she was at least five years older than the other girl, Celia's remark had still had the power to strike a raw nerve. 'No,' she answered quietly. 'No, I don't. I'm afraid I must seem a very dull creature compared to your friends.'

'Oh, don't be silly!' Celia touched her sleeve in protest, and Antonia guessed she had not intended to sound patronising. 'But as you do go out so seldom, surely you'd enjoy a party, just for once! I mean, you wouldn't have to stay long, if you didn't want to. Just come and have a drink and wish Reed and me well.'

Antonia sighed. 'Oh——'

'You'll come?' Celia took her indecision as a sign that she was weakening. 'Of course, you will.' Her warm smile appeared again. 'Make it about eight-thirty, or thereabouts. There'll be some food of sorts, if you're hungry, and Daddy's promised me at least a dozen bottles of champagne!'.

Once inside her apartment, Antonia leaned back against the door with some misgivings. She should have been more decisive, she thought impatiently. She should have refused Celia's invitation outright, instead of allowing the other girl to think she might change her mind. How could she go to their party? She didn't know anyone, except Celia, of course. And besides, they were not her sort of people. Even Uncle Harry did not have Mercedes' and Lamborghinis parked at his door.

Shaking her head, she pushed herself away from the panels and walked resolutely through the small living room and into the kitchen. Unpacking her shopping on to the drainer, she determinedly put all thoughts of the following evening's activities out of her head. Concentrating instead on an examination of what she had bought, she quickly disposed of her groceries into the fitted cupboards, and then plugged in the kettle.

Pausing in the doorway to the living room, she surveyed her surroundings without emotion. When she had first seen the apartment, it had been unfurnished, and the rooms had seemed bigger then. Now, with her mother's comfortable, chintz-covered sofa and arm-chairs taking up most of the space, there was hardly room for the gate-legged table she ate from. But then, her mother's furniture had been bought to furnish a generously proportioned four-bedroomed semi, not a single person's flat.

It was after six o'clock, she saw, with some surprise, the mellow rays of evening sunlight striking the face of the square carriage clock that stood on the mantelpiece. The apartments were centrally heated, but the old-fashioned fireplace still remained in Antonia's living room, modernised now by the addition of a rather ugly electric fire.

However, it was not the incongruity of the heating system that concerned her now. She must have spent longer with Celia than she had thought. Her mother would have been expecting her to ring at six o'clock, as usual, and abandoning any thought of dinner for the moment, Antonia picked up the phone.

These bi-weekly calls to Newcastle were going to prove expensive, Antonia reflected now, as she dialled her mother's number, but they were the only way she could keep in touch with Susie. Letters were not a satisfactory means of expression to an almost six-year-old, particularly one who found it hard to understand why her mother should have to go so far away to work. It simply wasn't enough to say there were no suitable jobs in Newcastle. Susie wanted to know why, if her mother had to live in London, she couldn't do so as well.

Mrs Lord answered the phone after the first couple of rings, and over her: 'Hello, Antonia? Is that you?' the protesting sound of Susie's voice was clearly audible.

'Yes, Mum, it's me,' Antonia answered ruefully, guessing her daughter was being quite a handful. 'I'm sorry I'm late. I was talking to one of the girls who lives upstairs.'

'You were? *Susie, behave yourself!* How nice, dear,' her mother responded disjointedly. 'But otherwise, you're all right, are you? Have you had a good week?'

'A busy one,' conceded Antonia, sinking down onto the arm of the sofa close by. 'Mr Fenwick has been away, and I've had to handle any emergencies myself.'

'Really? *Susie, put Tuppence down, there's a good girl!* They must have confidence in you then.'

'Not necessarily.' Antonia's tone was dry. 'But there is no one else, is there? Except Tom Brandon, of course, and he won't do anything he's not being paid for.' She paused, and then added reluctantly: 'I gather Susie's playing up again.'

'Oh, you know she has these phases,' exclaimed Mrs Lord tolerantly. 'Perhaps I'd better let her speak to you. There'll be no peace for either of us until I do.'

Antonia felt the familiar constriction in her throat when she heard her daughter's voice. She missed Susie terribly. Not just her company, and the mischief she got up to, but also her untidyness—the simple absence of anybody's occupation of the apartment but her own. At home, she had seemed to spend her time clearing up after the child, and she remembered grumbling about doing so. Now, she would have welcomed the activity with open arms.

'Are you being a good girl?' she asked Susie now, after the initial greetings were over. 'I can hear what's going on, you know. While Nanna was talking to me, you were making a nuisance of yourself, weren't you?'

'No.' Susie spoke with the convincing logic of someone who didn't regret her actions.

'But you were tormenting Tuppence, weren't you? You know she doesn't like being picked up.'

'Tuppence is fat!' declared Susie irrelevantly, as if the cat's weight had anything to do with it. Then, her voice taking on a heartbreakingly tearful note, she added: 'When are you coming to see me, Mummy? I don't like staying here with Nanna. Nanna won't play games with me like you do, and I don't like watching television.'

'Oh, Susie!' Antonia pressed her lips together tightly, fighting back a similar kind of emotion. This was the first time she and her daughter had been parted. When Simon walked out, she had worried for a time that he might try and take the child away from her, but her fears had proved groundless. Now, she had done what she had always declared she would never do: leave Susie without either of her parents.

'Couldn't I come and stay with you?' persisted the little girl now, taking her mother's prolonged silence as an encouraging sign, and Antonia hated to have to disappoint her.

'Darling, you have to go to school,' she said, choosing her words with care. 'And you have to take care of Nanna, too. She wouldn't like to live in that big old house on her own.'

Susie sniffed mutinously. 'Nanna wouldn't mind . . .'

'Yes, she would.'

'. . . and I could go to school in London, couldn't I?' she added reasonably.

Antonia shook her head. 'And what would you do when you came home from school and I wasn't here?' she asked gently. 'Susie, you know if there was any way we could be together, we would be so.' She hesitated. 'You know I'll be home for your birthday in two weeks time.'

Susie sniffed again. 'Why can't you come tonight? It's Friday. You don't work on Saturdays and Sundays, do you?'

'Well . . . no . . .'

'There you are then!'

'. . . but it would be too expensive,' explained Antonia, sighing. 'Darling, the train fare to Newcastle costs too much for Mummy to come and see you every weekend.'

There was more of the same, and then when Susie finally dissolved into tears as she usually did, Mrs Lord came back on the line. 'Don't worry, Antonia,' she assured her daughter airily, 'five minutes after I've put down this receiver, Susie will have forgotten all about it. And Howard and Sylvia are coming tomorrow, so she'll have the twins to play with.'

'Yes.' Antonia wished she felt more enthusiastic about that. Her brother's twin boys were seven years old, and in her experience Susie had never looked forward to their advent. Still . . .

'Don't worry, Antonia,' said her mother again, more brusquely now. 'Look, my dear, I've got to go. Susie has to have her bath yet, and I haven't fed Tuppence, and . . . and . . .'

'And it's Friday night,' remarked Antonia, with controlled irony. 'I know.' Her mother usually played bridge on Friday evenings. 'Okay, Mum. I'll ring again on Monday as usual.'

With the receiver replaced on its rest, Antonia found her will to go and make herself something to eat had been sadly diminished. The kettle had switched itself off in her absence, and allowing herself to slide disconsolately off the arm of the sofa, she subsided on to the cushioned seat. She always had this awful sense of emptiness after speaking to her mother and Susie, and it was incredibly difficult not to give way to a totally selfish desire to burst into tears.

But self-pity was not something she allowed herself to indulge in for long, and presently Antonia got up from the couch and went to make a cup of tea. A pizza she had bought in the supermarket on her way home, was soon heated under the grill, and putting her cup and plate on a tray, she carried them back into the living room.

The portable black-and-white television her mother had insisted she brought from home to keep her company held no interest for her, and propping the paperback novel she was presently reading on the cushions beside her, she tried to become involved with its cardboard characters. But it was no use. Susie's face kept intruding, and after eating half the pizza, Antonia put the book aside and turned on the radio.

The music programme she tuned into was soothing, and depositing the tray on the floor, Antonia curled her long legs up beside her. Had she really done the right thing by taking this job? she asked herself, for the umpteenth time, feeling the familiar sense of melancholy stealing over her. Was the fact that she had been looking for suitable employment for over three years a reasonable excuse for accepting a position so far from home? Uncle Harry, her mother's brother, had certainly thought so; but then, he had done the same more than twenty years ago, so he was biased.

'It's not as if you're a slip of a lass,' he had remarked candidly, when he drove up to Newcastle to offer her this flat. He was referring to Antonia's height of five feet eight inches, of course, and to the fact that she was five years past her twenty-first birthday. 'And you have been married,' he added, as if that was some further qualification. 'Your mother won't have to worry that you'll get yourself into trouble, if you see what I mean.'

Antonia did see, and Uncle Harry's words were valid. Her marriage to—and subsequent divorce from—Simon, had certainly taught her to be wary of the opposite sex. But as she had no intention of allowing any emotional relationship to develop, he could have saved his breath. Once bitten, twice shy, she quoted a little bitterly. She was free now, and self-supporting. No man was worth the sacrifice of surrendering those basic liberties.

Saturday was not one of Antonia's favourite days of the week. It was the day she cleaned the flat for a start and, like Sunday, it was inclined to drag. Uncle Harry, who lived in Wimbledon, had suggested she should go to them on Sundays, for lunch, but Antonia did not think it was fair on Aunt Mary. Their own two sons, and their wives and families, often turned up for lunch on Sundays, and although that first lonely weekend in London Antonia had taken them up on their offer, she had felt an intruder. They had tried to make her feel at home, but they had their own lives, their own friends; people they could talk about, but who meant nothing to her. After several awkward interludes, when Antonia had been excluded from their conversation, an awkward silence had fallen, and Antonia had never repeated the experience.

Perhaps she was too sensitive, she thought wearily, as she was vacuuming her bedroom. Perhaps if she had gone every Sunday, she would eventually have fitted in to their lives. The trouble was, they had not known what to say to her, beyond asking about her mother and Susie. The subject of Simon was apparently taboo, and when she would have explained that she had long recovered from the effects of his rejection, Aunt Mary had steered the conversation into other channels.

Later that afternoon, as she sat in an armchair drinking a well-earned cup of tea, she became aware of the sound of furniture being shifted in the room above. Apparently, Celia and her friend were getting ready for the party, Antonia reflected, half-enviously. It was years since she had attended anything but family get-togethers. Her marriage to Simon had cut her off from all her college friends, and when they split up, it simply wasn't possible to pick up the threads of her social life as if nothing had happened. Besides, there had been Susie to consider, and Antonia had tried to keep her life as stable as possible. But, after the divorce, the house she and Simon had bought with their savings had had to be sold, and Antonia had had no choice but to take her mother's advice and go back to living with her.

Realising she was allowing herself to sink into a state of depression, Antonia got up from her chair and carried her cup into the kitchen. Then, flexing her aching shoulders, she walked into the tiny bathroom that adjoined her bedroom. Turning on the bath taps, she squeezed some scented bath gel into the water, and then turned back into the bedroom to find herself some clean underwear.

Ten minutes later she was soaking in the deliciously perfumed water, feeling the tensions she had been experiencing easing out of her. Even the uncertain weather beyond her windows, that sent raindrops pattering against the pane, no longer had the power to depress her, and she relaxed lazily, allowing her thoughts to drift.

Perhaps she should go to the party, she mused reflectively. After all, she had been invited, and she didn't want to offend Celia. She was a nice girl, and she hoped she would be happy. No doubt this young man of hers—what was his name? Reed . . . Gallagher? No doubt, he was capable of supporting her in the manner to which she was accustomed. Celia would never be expected to do her own housework, or look after her own children, not unless she wanted to, of course. Antonia already knew that Mrs Francis paid a twice-weekly visit to the apartment upstairs: *Just to give the place the once-over!* as she put it; and whenever there was to be a party, the catering van from a very exclusive establishment was generally to be seen outside.

The water was cooling by the time she got out of the

bath, and after drying herself vigorously to restore her circulation, Antonia slipped on the pink towelling bathrobe her mother had bought for her at Christmas. Her hair needed drying, and collecting the hand-drier from the cupboard, Antonia seated herself in front of the dressing-table mirror. Removing the towel she had wound around her head while she got dry, she surveyed her reflection wryly. At least, she had no problems about what to do with her damp hair, she thought, tugging a brush through the damp strands. Shoulder-length and straight, it defied any attempt she made to put curl into it; and although once she had gone so far as to try perming, the result had been so awful, she had never tried again.

Dry, the toffee-brown ends tipped silkily against her shoulders. Combed from a centre parting, the two shining swathes framed the oval contours of her face, a feathery fringe brushing eyebrows that were several shades darker. Examining her skin for any unsightly blemish, Antonia had to admit that the polluted air of London had done nothing to mar it. Hazel eyes, which could look green in some lights, looked back at her from between her lashes, their slightly elongated shape giving her face a mildly interesting look. She was not beautiful; she knew that. Although she had good bone structure, her mouth was too wide, the lower lip too full. In the early days of their relationship, Simon used to say she had a sexy face, but she had long since dismissed any claims he made. Simon had wanted to get her into bed, and he had succeeded. The result had been Susie, and the rest was history.

Abandoning this particular train of thought, Antonia got up from the mirror and expelled her breath heavily. What was she going to do? she asked herself. Go to the party; or consign herself to another night of self-recrimination? She was becoming far too morose and introspective, she thought; and dull, painfully dull! Just because she had had one bad experience, she was allowing its aftermath to colour her whole outlook on life. All right, so she didn't want to get involved ever again. She didn't have to. She could still enjoy a party, with no strings attached.

The problem of what she was going to wear if she did go loomed next on her horizon. What did one wear to an informal party of this kind? She could wear jeans, she supposed, or cotton trousers; but as she wasn't absolutely sure how informal *informal* was, she decided it would be safer to stick with a skirt.

The fitted wardrobe easily accommodated her clothes with room to spare. One advantage of not leading a hectic social life was that one had less reason to buy expensive outfits, and Antonia's needs were not extensive. She generally wore a suit or a tailored dress to the office, and casual wear at other times. In consequence, what choice she had was limited, and she doubted there was anything to completely suit her purpose.

A pretty green batiste dress was appealing, but it seemed too summery for an April evening. A cotton two-piece was discarded for similar reasons, and the dark brown corded trouser suit, which always looked good, was dismissed on two counts: it was too warm to wear indoors, and it didn't have a skirt.

Sighing, Antonia eventually pulled out the only item she might regard as wearable. It was a cream shirt-waisted dress, with full sleeves and a narrow skirt, that ended just above her knees. Made of Thai silk, she had bought it in a sale in Newcastle the previous January, and since then, she had simply not had an occasion to wear it. Even in the sale, it had not been cheap, and her mother had thought her quite mad to spend her money on one item when she might have had two. Now, however, Antonia knew it was exactly what she was looking for, and stripping off the bathrobe, she put it on.

She had never realised how flattering the colour was, she thought, lifting her hair out of the neckline and turning this way and that. The low vee in front drew attention to the enticing swell of her breasts, and for once she did not deplore their fullness. Since having

Susie, her breasts had become heavier, and she had seen
no advantages in the contrast they posed to the
narrowness of her waist. Now, however, she saw that
the dusky hollow just visible above the buttons of the
dress was not unappealing, and her lips parted a little
wryly at her unwarranted enthusiasm. What did it
matter what she looked like, after all? She wasn't going
to the party in the hope of attracting some man.
Nevertheless, there was a certain satisfaction to be
found in knowing she was looking her best, and she was
still woman enough not to want Celia to go on feeling
sorry for her.

When she left her flat at eight-thirty to climb the
stairs to the apartment upstairs, she joined several other
young people, evidently with the same destination. But
they were not on their own, as she was. They were in
groups of two or three, all laughing and talking
together, with the easy cameraderie of long practice.
They cast faintly speculative glances in Antonia's
direction—not unfriendly actually, but not specially
kind—and one or two of the young men eyed her with a
more than passing interest. But generally they all
regarded her with some curiosity, and Antonia became
increasingly convinced she should not have come.
Perhaps if she turned round now, she thought, having
reached the first floor landing where the buzz of music
and conversation coming through the open door of the
apartment was quite overpowering. Who would notice?
she asked herself. Who would care? But the realisation
that she would have to run the gauntlet of several more
people climbing the stairs behind her drove her on, and
because she had no alternative, she was obliged to take
the plunge.

At least, what she was wearing was acceptable, she
mused, with some relief. Although it was raining
outside, it was not a cold evening, and she had seen one
or two girls wearing dresses similar to her own. There
were girls in trousers, but not as many as she might
have expected, and the men's clothes reflected their
girlfriends' casual tastes.

It soon became apparent that the apartment Celia and her friend occupied was approximately twice the size of Antonia's. Unlike the floor below, which was divided into two flats—the other being occupied by the caretaker and his wife—the first floor was given over entirely to the apartment leased by the two girls. Halting on the threshold of a warmly lit entrance hall, Antonia was immediately impressed by an atmosphere redolent with the mingled scents of expensive perfumes, Havana tobacco, and fine wines; and she didn't need to see the banks of flowers or feel her feet sinking into the Persian carpet to know that everything Mrs Francis had hinted must be true.

Ahead of her, the young men and girls who had preceded her up the stairs were soon absorbed into the welcoming surge of people swelling through the matching doors that gave access to the living room. The amplified projection of the song that was presently topping the popular music charts made any formal introductions impossible, and the couple behind Antonia were compelling her to move forward. Almost without her own volition, she was propelled through the doors, and was soon engulfed by that noisy jostling throng.

The room was literally full of people, spilling over the arms of brocade-covered sofas and squashy leather armchairs on to stools and bean-filled cushions, and even the floor. The living room was large by anybody's standards, but although Antonia had heard of its silk-hung walls and high moulded ceilings from Mrs Francis, it was difficult to appreciate its elegance tonight. The rhythm emanating from the hi-fi system and its accompanying speakers created a constant vibration, and the smoke from more than a dozen cheroots and cigarettes was sending a hazy cloud drifting irresistibly upwards. Those people who had just arrived, or perhaps those who simply preferred to circulate, made up the relaxed gathering that swelled from the entrance into the middle of the floor; and Antonia found herself a part of that gathering; anxious, and decidedly *not* relaxed. Where was Celia? she wondered, turning on heels that were a little higher than she usually wore. Surely she had to be here somewhere! But where?

'Are you looking for somebody in particular, or will I do?' enquired an attractive male voice close to her ear, and Antonia swung round with incautious haste to face the questioner. Incautious, because her heel caught in the shaggy pile of the carpet, and had her inquisitor not been there to grab at, she might easily have disgraced herself completely and landed at his feet.

Instead, she clutched rather wildly for his arm, her grappling fingers barely registering the subtle softness of his suede-covered sleeve. As she struggled to disentangle her heel from its infuriating cohesion with the carpet, she was scarcely aware of him using his free hand to help her regain her balance until, in doing so, he brought her up against the lean hardness of his body. Then, as her heel came loose, she was able to look up at him, and the humorous gleam in his grey eyes made her quickly put some space between them.

'I'm sorry,' she said, colouring hotly as she apprehended what had happened. 'I caught my heel . . .'

'I know.' The amused grey eyes were regarding her with frank appreciation. 'But I guess I was responsible. I did attract your attention.'

'It was you . . .'

'. . . who spoke to you? Yes, it was.' He smiled, his lips parting to reveal even white teeth. 'You looked—lost. I wanted to help you.'

'Not bring me to my knees?' countered Antonia wryly, the humour of the situation restoring her composure. 'Well—thank you, anyway. I'm all right.'

'I'm pleased to hear it.' But he did not move away as she had expected. Instead, he collected two long-stemmed glasses of a beige, bubbling liquid, from a tray being held by a passing waiter, and handed one to her. 'Be my guest!'

Antonia took the glass reluctantly, but a surreptitious glance about her assured her that their exchange was not attracting any unnecessary attention. On the contrary, the music and the buzz of conversation was going on as before, and it was only in her mind that she and this man who had rescued her from instant ignominy had isolated themselves from the rest.

Licking an errant drop of champagne—for that was what it was, she realised—from her lips, she cast covert eyes in his direction. Disconcertingly, he was watching her, but that didn't prevent her hastily averted gaze from noticing how attractive he was. Straight dark hair, rather longer than was fashionable; a lean, narrow-boned face; skin that still bore the tan of a winter holiday; even without the fact that he could look down at her from the advantage of at least three inches, notwithstanding her high heels, he was a disturbing man. But it was his eyes that really disrupted her carefully composed indifference; grey, as she already knew, they were fringed by thick straight lashes, that gave a wholly sensual appeal to an otherwise ascetically handsome face.

'Do you like it?' he enquired lazily, and Antonia controlled her colour with difficulty.

'Like what?' she asked, rather too sharply for politeness.

'Why—the champagne, of course,' he replied smoothly, and Antonia concentrated on the wine in her glass to avoid his knowing gaze.

'It's—very nice,' she answered, determinedly taking another sip. It was infuriating, but he was making her feel as gauche as a schoolgirl, and she had to remind herself that she was a divorcee with a six-year-old daughter.

'You're different from what I expected,' he remarked suddenly, surprising her into looking at him again. 'Cee said you were shy and rather ordinary. But you're not. Though I suppose another female might not realise it.'

Antonia caught her breath. 'Has she been discussing me with her friends? Is that why she invited me here? To satisfy their curiosity?'

Her voice had risen slightly as she spoke, and the

CHAPTER TWO

ANTONIA's office adjoined that of Martin Fenwick's. It wasn't much of an office really, just a desk and a chair and a filing cabinet, in a room large enough to accommodate them and her, but at least it offered her some privacy. And her work was interesting.

Seven years ago, when she had had to give up all thoughts of a career to have Susie, she had been in the second year of a sociology degree at Durham university. Working *with* people and *for* the community had always interested her, and her intention had been to try and get a job in some branch of the social services. But Simon's advent into her life had interrupted her plans, and afterwards, when she had found it necessary to look for work, her qualifications were sadly limited. Of course, had she had the money, she could have returned to university as a mature student and taken up her studies again, but that was out of the question with Susie to support. Instead, she had applied for any job that had offered the chance of working in a similar field, and in spite of its disadvantages in terms of distance, she had been delighted to accept her present position.

The institute, where she worked as Assistant to the Director, was an independently operated youth training establishment, offering skills in various manual trades, as well as academic qualifications. Courses in book-keeping and accountancy, shorthand and typewriting, competed with mechanical engineering and carpentry, and the students were encouraged to try more than one course before deciding on the one that suited them best.

Antonia considered herself very fortunate to have been offered the post, and she felt she owed a debt to her past tutor at Durham for giving him his backing and support. Without the reference he had been able to supply, she felt sure she would not have been so lucky, and the doubts she had had about leaving the north of England had been stifled by the faith he had had in her.

To her relief Mr Fenwick, who had been absent the previous week due to an apparently seasonal attack of lumbago, was back at work on Monday morning, and Antonia was able to return to her own duties. Her experience at the job had not yet equipped her to handle all the hundred and one little problems that could occur in the course of a working week, and there were several outstanding difficulties she was going to have to discuss with him when he had the time.

But to begin with, the institute's director had enough to do handling the enormous backlog of mail, which had required his personal attention, and Antonia spent most of Monday morning trying to catch up on her own duties.

Even so, she did not find it easy to apply herself to practical matters. It wasn't that her work was difficult or anything. It was simply that her mind kept drifting away from what she was doing, and several times she found herself staring into space, totally detached from her surroundings.

It was the remembrance of Saturday night that was troubling her, of course. The party, which she had not wanted to attend, and which was now lodged painfully in her memory. Just thinking of that scene in Celia's living room caused Antonia's face to flood with colour, and it still amazed her that she had stayed so long when all she had really wanted to do was escape.

She should have made her apologies as soon as a decent interval had elapsed, she thought, and hurried back to her own apartment. Certainly, Celia's flatmate, the *Honourable* Elizabeth, *Liz*, Ashford, had thought so. It had soon become apparent that the other occupant of the first floor apartment did not share her friend's enthusiasm to mix with their neighbours, and her greeting had been distant, to say the least. The other female guests seemed to take their lead from her, and regarded Antonia with something less than cordiality,

and it was left to Celia and the male contingent to try
and put her at her ease.

That it hadn't worked was mainly due to Antonia's
own behaviour. She had not come to the party to be
propositioned, and she was not used to finding herself
the centre of attraction. Besides, if she was honest she
would admit that the awareness of Reed Gallagher in
the background, watching her embarrassed attempts to
break free of her admirers, had coloured her attitude
towards them, and what might have been an amusing
situation turned into a trial of nerves.

Learning that the man she had been so arbitrarily
crossing swords with was really Celia's fiancé had been
a shock. Not that she had any interest in him
personally, she assured herself, but his attitude towards
her had not been that of a man desperately in love with
his fiancée. At least, not in her experience it hadn't.
Perhaps their sort of people behaved differently.
Perhaps, even in this day and age, it was to be a
marriage engineered for convenience. But then, remembering the way Celia had clung to her fiancé's arm
and the adoring looks she had cast in his direction,
Antonia felt convinced that for her part, Celia cared
madly for her handsome Irishman. And probably he
did, too, she reflected cynically, refusing to admit that
initially she, too, had been disarmed. Whatever his
feelings, she was unlikely to discover them, though she
had the distinct suspicion he was not as careless and
superficial as he would have had her believe. And when
he had taken hold of her wrist . . .

Shaking her head to dislodge the irritating recollection
of the cool strength of Reed's fingers against her skin,
Antonia endeavoured to apply herself to the application
forms in front of her. The institute was always
oversubscribed on all their courses, and it was to be
part of her duties to consider each application on its
merit, and winnow them down to a more manageable
thirty-five or forty from which Mr Fenwick could make
his final choice. New trainees were admitted in
September, and interviews were apparently held in May

and June to reduce the eventual intake to approximately twenty in each department. It promised to be an interesting part of her work, particularly as Mr Fenwick had informed her that in his opinion aptitude for a particular occupation was worth more than any number of academic qualifications.

This morning, however, Antonia's brain refused to function, and by eleven o'clock she was still studying the second form. When Martin Fenwick appeared to ask her to come into his office, she abandoned her task with a feeling of relief, following him into his room with an enthusiasm untempered by her usual impatience to get on with her own job.

Blowing his nose before taking his seat, her boss regarded her rather speculatively. 'Are you feeling all right, Mrs Sheldon?' he asked, gesturing her to a chair on the other side of his desk. 'You're looking rather tired. Did you go home at the weekend?'

Not entirely relishing his probably well-meant enquiry, Antonia shook her head. 'If you mean to Newcastle—then, no,' she answered politely, wondering if she had bags under her eyes. 'I . . . er . . . didn't sleep very well last night.'

Martin Fenwick nodded. 'I haven't been sleeping too well myself,' he confessed, sinking down into his chair. 'Lumbago's the devil of a thing. Wakes you up, every time you turn over.'

'I'm sorry.' Antonia summoned a small smile. 'But you're feeling better now.'

'Well—it's bearable,' he essayed heavily, shuffling the papers on his desk. 'I suppose at my age I have to expect something. Be thankful yours is not a chronic condition.'

'Yes.'

Antonia conceded his point, although lying awake in the early hours it had felt very much as though it was. She had blamed the fact that on Sunday she had done nothing but laze around the flat, but that wasn't entirely true either. What she was really doing was coming to terms with the rather unpalatable realisation that in spite of her unfortunate experience with Simon, she was still not immune to sexual attraction.

'So—shall we get down to business?' suggested Mr Fenwick now, smoothing one hand over his bald pate as he read through the report she had prepared for him. 'This is good, very good. Very comprehensive.' His slightly rheumy eyes twinkled as he looked up at her. 'I knew you were the woman for the job, as soon as I set eyes on you.'

Antonia was grateful for his confidence, and she did her best to satisfy all his enquiries, and learn how to deal with problems in his absence in the process. The failure of the hydraulic lift in the motor repair workshop had caused her some difficulties, she confessed, and the trainee joiner who had cut his hand badly on an electric saw deserved a reprimand she had not felt able to give him. Nevertheless, on the whole, there had been no insurmountable set-backs, and she knew by the end of their discussion that Mr Fenwick felt his belief in her abilities had been justified.

The afternoon proved rather less traumatic. After a snack lunch in the dining hall with Heather Jakes, Mr Fenwick's secretary, Antonia returned to her desk to find her concentration was much improved. Determining not to waste any more time weighing the pros and cons of her attendance at the party, she put all thoughts of Celia Lytton-Smythe and her fiancé aside, and applied herself instead to the relative merits of a certificate in woodwork and an ability to type.

It was nearing six o'clock when Antonia reached the stone gate-posts that marked the boundary of Eaton Lodge. She had been grateful to find there was a short drive leading up to the house. Her rooms, being on the ground floor, would have adjoined the street otherwise, and she was still not accustomed to the sound of traffic at all hours of the day and night. Her mother's house, in a suburb of Newcastle, was situated in a quiet cul-de-sac, and it had not been easy for her to make the transition.

Even so, she was glad that she did not have expensive

train fares to add to her living expenses. The flat, in Clifton Gate, was only a bus ride from the institute in the Edgware Road, and on summer days she planned to walk to and from work. The exercise would do her good, and the resultant savings might enable her to pay more frequent visits to Newcastle—and Susie.

As she walked up the short path to the house, the black Lamborghini overtook her, and for the first time she saw Reed Gallagher at the wheel. It was early for him, she thought, aware of an unwelcome tightening of her stomach muscles. She couldn't remember seeing the car in the drive much before seven-thirty or eight o'clock in the past, though she had to admit that until Celia pointed it out, she had paid little attention to their visitors. Now, however, she was all too aware of its occupant, and it took a certain amount of stamina to continue up the drive as if nothing untoward had happened.

By the time she reached the entrance, Reed had parked the powerful sports car, crossed the forecourt, and was waiting for her. In a dark blue three-piece business suit and a white shirt, he looked little different from the less formally dressed individual she had met at the party. With a conservative tie narrowly concealing the buttons of his shirt, and his hands pushed carelessly into the pockets of his jacket, he appeared relaxed and self-assured, confident in his cool male arrogance—and Antonia resented his somehow insolent supposition that she might be pleased to exchange a few words with him.

'Hi,' he said, as she came up the steps, his lean frame successfully blocking her passage. 'How are you?'

Antonia held up her head and without looking at him, made her intentions evident. 'I'm fine, thank you, Mr Gallagher,' she responded stiffly, edging towards the door. 'Do you mind?'

Reed regarded her steadily for a few moments—she could almost *feel* those disturbing grey eyes probing her averted lids—then he politely stepped aside. 'My pleasure,' he assured her, allowing her to precede him into the gloomy entrance hall. 'It's cold out tonight, isn't it? *Very* chilly!'

Pressing her lips together to suppress the immature retort that sprang into her mind, Antonia rummaged in her handbag for her key. If only she'd thought to do this before she came inside, she thought frustratedly. It was difficult to see what she was doing without the benefit of a light.

Aware that Reed had not continued on upstairs as she had expected, her fingers were all thumbs, and when she eventually found the key, it slithered annoyingly out of her grasp. With a little ping, it landed on the floor at Reed's feet, and with a feeling of helplessness, she watched him bend and rescue it for her with a lithe graceful movement.

'Let me,' he said, avoiding her outstretched hand, and she stood stiffly by as he inserted the key in the lock and deftly turned the handle. 'No problem,' he added, dropping the key into her palm, and knowing she was behaving badly, but unable to do anything about it, Antonia gave him a curt nod before scurrying into the flat.

She was still leaning back against the closed door, her heart beating rather faster than was normal, when she heard the brisk tattoo on the panels behind her. Realising it could be no one else but him, she was tempted to pretend she hadn't heard his knock, but she knew that would be childish. There was no likelihood that she might not have heard his summons, and by not answering her door she would look as if she was afraid to do so.

Taking a deep breath, she gathered together the two sides of her camel-hair jacket, which she had just unbuttoned, and turned. With carefully schooled features, she swung open the door again, holding on to the handle, as if there was any chance that he might try to force himself inside.

Reed was leaning against the wall to one side of the door, but when she looked out he straightened, and turned to face her. 'Yes?' she said tersely, unable to keep the hostility out of her voice, and his dark features took on a rueful aspect.

'Can I come in?'

Antonia could not have been more surprised, and it showed. 'I beg your pardon . . .'

'I said, can I come in?' he repeated levelly, glancing over her shoulder into the small apartment. 'I want to talk to you, and I'd prefer not to do so in Mrs Francis's hearing.'

'Mrs Francis?' Antonia's tongue circled her lips, and Reed nodded.

'Any minute now, her door is going to open—just a crack,' he confided drily. 'So?'

Antonia cast a half-glance behind her, suddenly conscious of the enormous contrast between her modest apartment and the luxurious rooms occupied by his fiancée. And she realised she didn't want him to see where she lived. She didn't want him coming into her flat, comparing her shabby furnishings with the designer fabrics upstairs. This was her home, such as it was, and she didn't want his disruptive influence invading its sanctuary.

'I don't think that's a very good idea,' she said now, endeavouring to maintain a politely indifferent tone. 'I can't think of anything we have to say to one another, Mr Gallagher. If Celia's not at home, I'm sorry, but I'm afraid you can't wait here.'

Reed expelled his breath noisily. 'I don't know if Cee's at home or not,' he retorted, his lean face losing its humorous expression. 'Look—I'm not about to ravage you or anything. I simply wanted to apologise if you think I was indiscreet.'

Antonia looked at him unwillingly, her diffident gaze drawn to the clean-cut lines of his face. 'Indiscreet?'

'By telling you what Cee had said,' he inserted flatly. 'And by not telling you who I was.'

Antonia's nostrils flared, ever so slightly. 'It's not important . . .'

'I think it is.'

'Why?' Her fingers tightened on the metal handle. 'We are hardly likely to meet again, are we?'

'Why not?' The long straight lashes narrowed his eyes. 'Cee likes you. She told me.' He paused, and when she made no response, he added: 'Well—I guess that's all I came to say.'

Antonia drew an unsteady breath. 'Is it?' she murmured, her long fingers fidgeting with the collar of her coat. Suddenly, she was disappointed. 'I—is your fiancée at home?'

Reed glanced carelessly up the stairs. 'I doubt it,' he responded, pulling one hand out of his pocket and combing his fingers through the dark vitality of his hair. 'The shop doesn't close until six, and it's barely that now. But don't worry about it,' he finished with some irony. 'I have a key.'

Antonia hesitated. 'I—I was just going to make some tea,' she offered, regretting the words almost as soon as they were uttered. Whatever had possessed her to offer him her hospitality? she asked herself impatiently. Did she want him carrying tales upstairs of the straightened circumstances in which she lived? 'I mean,' she added awkwardly, 'I don't suppose you—drink tea.'

'Well, I don't survive on honeydew and nectar,' he responded, his grey eyes gently teasing. 'Thank you, Miss Sheldon. I'd love a cup of tea.'

She had to step aside then, and treading silently on suede-booted feet, Reed entered the flat. Unlike the apartment occupied by Celia and her friend, there was no entrance hall. One stepped directly into Antonia's living room, and her colour deepened embarrassingly as Reed looked about him with evident interest.

With the door closed behind him, Antonia did not linger to correct his assumption of her status. Shedding her coat on to a chair as she passed, she walked through the living room into the kitchen, leaving him to make what he liked of the flat. She simply wasn't interested, she told herself, filling the kettle at the tap and pushing in the electric plug. The sooner he had his tea and departed, the better. And after all, Celia might not approve of his making a detour, when he was evidently on his way to visit her.

She was examining the contents of the biscuit tin when his shadow fell across her. 'A watched pot never boils, isn't that what they say?' he remarked drily, surveying the pristine neatness of the kitchen. 'Come and sit down. You must be tired.'

'Do I look tired?'

After what Mr Fenwick had said earlier, Antonia's tone was unnecessarily tense, and Reed regarded her with rueful tolerance. 'I guess I always seem to say the wrong thing, don't I?' he averred, running a lazy hand around the back of his neck. 'Now, how can I redeem myself? By telling you I was only being polite, or by assuring you that you look pretty good to me?'

Antonia bent her head. 'Neither. It doesn't matter. I—you go and sit down. I'll join you presently.'

'Okay.'

With a careless shrug he left her, and Antonia took cups out of the cupboard above the drainer, and set them on their saucers. By the time she had put milk into a jug and set it, along with the sugar bowl, on a tray, the kettle had boiled. Filling the teapot, she put it on the tray, too, and then after checking she had everything, she carried it through to the living room.

Reed was lounging on the sofa, flicking through the pages of a self-help magazine she had bought to learn how to do minor repairs. In her absence, he had loosened the top two buttons of his shirt and pulled his tie a couple of inches below his collar, and the slightly dishevelled appearance suited him. But then, anything would, thought Antonia woodenly, refusing to respond to his lazy smile. He was vibrant; magnetic; the kind of man one could not help but be aware of, his unconscious sexuality a challenge in itself.

Conscious of this, she seated herself on the armchair opposite him, and made a play of pouring the tea. 'Milk and sugar?' she enquired, the jug poised just above the cup, but he shook his head, and responded lightly: 'As it is.'

Belatedly, she guessed he was used to taking it with lemon, but in any case, she didn't have any. And besides, her tea was not Lapsang or Orange Pekoe. It was just common-or-garden quick-brew that she bought at the supermarket.

Still, he seemed to enjoy it, resting his ankle across his knee, emptying his cup and accepting a second. She should have known he would feel at ease anywhere, she thought, going to cross her legs and then thinking better of it. Like a chameleon, he adapted to his surroundings, totally indifferent to anyone's feelings but his own. He was making her feel a stranger in her own apartment, and she resented his easy manner almost as much as his sex appeal.

'Why don't you like me, Miss Sheldon?' he asked suddenly, setting his cup back on the tray while Antonia's clattered noisily in its saucer. 'Do I frighten you? Is that it? Are you afraid of men, perhaps? I'd be interested to know what I've done to provoke such a reaction.'

Antonia replaced her cup on the table with rather more care than she had picked it up. 'I think you're imagining things, Mr Gallagher.'

'Am I?' His eyes were shrewdly assessing. 'We may not know one another very well—which I'm sure is your next line of defence—but I can sense hostility when I feel it, Miss Sheldon.'

'It's not—*Miss* Sheldon,' she corrected him abruptly. 'It's *Mrs* I am—I *was*—married.'

'Ah!'

His long-drawn sigh infuriated her, and abandoning any further attempt at politeness, she sprang to her feet. 'It's not what you're thinking, Mr Gallagher,' she declared hotly, her hands clenching and unclenching at her sides. 'I'm not *afraid* of the opposite sex. I don't hate all men, or anything like that. I simply—I simply don't care for . . . for men of your type, that's all!'

'My type?' he prompted softly, and she felt the instinctive thrill of knowing she was getting into deep water without any means of saving herself. 'Men like your ex-husband perhaps?'

Like Simon! Antonia knew an hysterical desire to

laugh. No one less like Simon could she imagine. Oh,
Simon himself might have seen himself as being
attractive to women, as knowing all the answers, but
compared to Reed Gallagher, he had only been an
amateur. And she had probably been at least partly
responsible for the high opinion Simon had had of
himself. Although it had meant giving up her degree at
university, she had been flattered that the local heart-
throb should have chosen her as his girlfriend, and she
had fallen for his good looks without ever questioning
what might lie beneath the surface. Until it was too late.

'You're nothing like my husband!' she retorted now,
suddenly losing enthusiasm for the argument. The
reason she resented Reed Gallagher had nothing to do
with Simon's defection, and she felt ridiculously gauche
for having lost her temper. 'I—I shouldn't have implied
that you were.'

Aware of her discomfort, Reed got resignedly to his
feet and tightened the knot of his tie once again. 'I
think I'd better go,' he remarked, stepping sideways
round the low table on which she had set the tray.
'Thanks for the tea. It was—delicious.'

Antonia was sure it had been nothing of the kind,
and her own behaviour had been unforgivable, but
there was nothing she could say. Short of offering an
apology, which she had no intention of doing, she could
only spare him a tight smile as he walked towards the
door, and with a knowing inclination of his head, he let
himself out of the flat.

Conversely, as soon as he had gone, Antonia wanted
to call him back. Sinking down on to the edge of her
chair, she cupped her chin in her hands and stared
humiliatedly at the spot on the sofa where he had been
sitting. What a fiasco! she thought bitterly. What an
absolute fool she had made of herself. She hadn't
wanted him to leave with that impression of her,
particularly not when she thought how amusing it
would seem when he related the incident to Celia—and
Liz.

The disturbing dampness of a tear sliding down to

touch her fingertips brought Antonia a measure of
relief. It *wasn't* that important, she told herself, dashing
the tear away and making a concerted effort to pull
herself together. Putting the teapot and her cup on to
the tray, she picked it up and carried it into the kitchen.
It wasn't as if she and Celia were close friends or
anything. It would teach her to be more wary of them
in future. They were not like her, and she should
remember that.

CHAPTER THREE

IT was over a week before Antonia encountered either of her upstairs neighbours again.

It had been an unsettled week for her, not helped by the discovery, when she came home from work on Tuesday evening, of the delicate bouquet of creamy narcissus, hazy blue irises and nodding yellow daffodils residing in her kitchen sink.

'I didn't know where else to put them,' declared Mrs Francis confidentially, knocking at her door only minutes after Antonia had arrived home to explain that she had taken delivery of the flowers. 'It seemed a shame to leave them lying in the hall,' she added, regarding her newest tenant with rather more interest than before. 'They're so beautiful, aren't they? You've evidently got an admirer, Mrs Sheldon.'

Antonia smiled, but her thoughts were not as tranquil as her expression. She had already perceived that there was no card with the flowers, and there was only one person in her estimation who could have sent them. Reed Gallagher.

'I—I'm very grateful, Mrs Francis,' she said now, hoping the garrulous caretaker's wife would not pursue the subject, but she was disappointed.

'I had to put them in the sink,' Mrs Francis, continued, looking beyond Antonia, into the living room. 'I . . . er . . . I didn't like to look for a vase, and as there were *so many* . . .'

'Yes. Well, thank you.' Antonia lifted her shoulders apologetically. 'I'll find something.'

'I could lend you a vase, or maybe two, if you need them,' offered Mrs Francis helpfully, but Antonia was adamant.

'I'm sure I can manage,' she refused politely, feeling distinctly mean for not satisfying the older woman's curiosity. But how could she tell Mrs Francis that Celia Lytton-Smythe's fiancé had sent her the flowers? How dare Reed Gallagher put her in this position?

'Well, if you're sure ...' Reluctantly, Mrs Francis was having to abandon her enquiries. 'You're a lucky girl!' she remarked, starting back across the hall. 'They must have cost someone a pretty penny.'

Antonia smiled again to soften her words. 'I'm sure they must,' she agreed, and closed the door firmly before any further comment could be made.

Nevertheless, as she filled every bowl and jug and milk bottle she possessed with the softly scented blossoms, Antonia couldn't help inhaling their delicious fragrance. She had never possessed so many flowers in her life before, and while her initial instinct had been to return the bouquet to its sender, the practicalities of such an action deterred her. For one thing, she had no idea where Reed Gallagher lived or worked, and even if she had, could she take the risk of embarrassing Celia should she be with him at the time? In addition to which, there was always the possibility—however slight—that Reed Gallagher might not have sent them. How ridiculous she would look if she returned the flowers to him and he knew nothing about them!

One final solution occurred, but it was one she did not consider for long. The idea of returning the flowers to the shop that had sent them did not appeal to her at all. She could not consign such delicate blooms to instant destruction, and besides, if Reed had sent the flowers anonymously, as she suspected, he might never learn of her sacrifice.

Stifling her conscience with this thought, she found she derived a great deal of pleasure from the colour they gave to her rather dull living room. Coming into the flat after a day's work, she found herself anticipating their vivid presence, and when they eventually began to fade, she bought herself some daffodils to mitigate their loss.

She spoke to Susie again on the phone, and promised her the days to her birthday would soon pass. 'I'll come on the six o'clock train next Friday evening,' she told her mother, a week before she was due to leave. 'I'm looking forward to it so much. It seems much more than eight weeks since I came to London.'

The weekend was uneventful. She guessed Celia and her friend must have gone away, for there was no sound from the apartment upstairs all Saturday and Sunday. Antonia spent the time giving her kitchen a brightening lick of paint, and determinedly avoiding the inevitable comparisons between this weekend and last.

On Monday evening, however, she came face to face with Celia in the entrance hall. The other girl was on her way out as she arrived home, and the bunch of daffodils in Antonia's hand drew Celia's attention.

'Aren't they lovely!' she exclaimed, bending her head to inhale their fragrance. 'I love spring flowers, don't you?' Then her eyes took on a mischievious glint. 'Of course, you do. Mrs Francis told me someone sent you absolutely loads of them!'

Antonia caught her breath. She should have realised that if Mrs Francis gossiped to her, she would gossip to her other tenants as well. 'Oh—yes,' she managed now. 'I . . . was rather fortunate. A . . . a friend from work. He . . . he sent them.'

Now why had she said that? she asked herself impatiently, as Celia nodded her head. Who at the institute was likely to send her flowers? And how could she be sure Reed hadn't confided his generosity to his fiancée?

'I love receiving flowers,' Celia was saying now, her words justifying Antonia's caution. 'Reed sends me roses all the time. He knows I love them.'

Antonia moistened her lips. 'You're very lucky.'

'Yes, I am.' Celia sighed contentedly, and Antonia felt the biggest bitch of all time. 'Did you see my ring?' She extended her hand. 'Isn't it gorgeous?'

It was. A large square-cut sapphire, surrounded by a cluster of diamonds, it glowed, even in the subdued light of the hall, and Antonia did not have to affect her admiration. 'It's beautiful,' she said, her smile warmly sincere. 'When . . . when are you getting married? Or haven't you decided yet?'

'In December, I think,' Celia replied, admiring the ring herself. 'Reed's pretty tied up until then, but I'm hoping we can have a Christmas honeymoon.'

'How nice.'

Antonia's tone was a little forced now, but Celia didn't seem to notice. 'Yes, isn't it?' she responded, lifting her shoulders. 'But now, enough about me, I've not seen you since the party: how did you enjoy it?'

'Oh——' Antonia swallowed. 'It was . . . very enjoyable. I'm sorry. I should have rung. But what with one thing and another——'

'Think nothing of it.' Celia shook her head dismissively. 'I just hoped you hadn't taken offence over the way Liz acted. She can be pretty bloody sometimes, and that was one of them. She's really quite charming, when you get to know her.'

Antonia cleared her throat. 'I—I'm sure she is. Really, it's not important. It was your night, after all.'

'What did you think of Reed?' asked Celia suddenly, and Antonia had the suspicion she had been leading up to this all along. 'You spoke with him, didn't you? Isn't he something?'

The daffodils slipped abruptly from Antonia's fingers, and in the confusion of bending to pick them up, Celia's question was left unanswered. 'I must go,' she said, her mind obviously already on other things. She glanced at her watch. 'I'm meeting Daddy in fifteen minutes, and he won't be very happy if I'm late. By—eee.'

'Goodbye.'

Antonia summoned a farewell smile, but after Celia had disappeared out the door, she felt a wave of weariness sweep over her. It seemed more than five years since she had been as young and vital as Celia, she thought. Had she *ever* been that young? she wondered wistfully.

Tuesday brought a spate of accidents at the institute. Heather Jakes stumbled up the steps that morning and sprained her wrist, thus preventing her from doing any typing that day; Mark Stephens, the caretaker, strained his back shifting boxes in the storeroom; and Mr Fenwick split his trousers on his way to work and in consequence, didn't appear at all until eleven o'clock.

'Probably due to all those marshmallows he keeps eating,' remarked Heather uncharitably, coming into Antonia's office to deliver the message. She held out her bandaged wrist for the other girl's inspection. 'It's just as well really. I can't do much with this.'

'No.' Antonia grimaced. 'I just hope Mr Stephens is all right, too. He's really too old to be lifting such heavy weights.'

'Tell that to the governors,' declared Heather airily, sauntering back to the door. 'They're all for keeping costs down, which in lay terms means employing fewer people. You don't know how lucky you were, getting this job!'

'Oh, I do.' Antonia spoke fervently. 'I have been looking for a job for a long time, Heather.'

'Hmm.' Heather shrugged. 'Well, I think it's a shame you had to leave your little girl in Newcastle. The powers that be should take things like that into consideration, when they offer a job to a woman.'

'Maybe one day I'll be able to afford to pay someone to take care of her, when she's not at school,' said Antonia, voicing her own private thoughts on the matter. 'Or perhaps, when she's older, and can take care of herself until I get home she can live with me.'

'Men never have these problems, do they?' Heather remarked drily. 'If they did, they'd soon find a way to deal with it.'

Antonia smiled. 'You sound aggressive. Have you had another row with Peter?'

'Not another row!' Heather laughed. 'Just the same one. He wants me to agree to give up *my* work if we have a baby.'

'And is that likely?'

'What? My giving up work? Not on your . . .'

'No. I mean the baby,' said Antonia gently. 'How long have you been married?'

'Two years,' Heather grimaced. 'And the answer is no, on both counts. Not so long as Peter insists on being such a chauvinist!'

By lunchtime, Antonia felt as if she had done a full day's work. There were certain letters that had to be attended to, and with Heather's incapacity, Antonia took it upon herself to do the typing. It wasn't easy. It was years since she had played about on an old typewriter of her father's, and Heather's sophisticated electric machine was unfamiliar to her. To begin with, she pressed too hard on the keys and had rows of letters appearing instead of just one, and when she did succeed in producing an acceptable copy, she discovered she had forgotten to put a carbon between the sheets.

With shopping to do in her lunch hour, she decided to miss out on the salad in the dining hall. Instead, she put on the jacket of her dark grey suit, ran a hasty comb through her hair, and emerged into the pale sunshine flooding the Edgware Road.

The sight of the black sports car, parked carelessly on the double yellow lines outside, would have alerted her, without the added identification of the man leaning casually against the bonnet. Reed Gallagher, for she had no difficulty in discerning his lean, sinuous frame, straightened abruptly at her appearance, and although she started swiftly away along the pavement, he had no problem in overtaking her.

'Hey,' he exclaimed, his hand on her sleeve barely slowing her progress. 'I was waiting for you.'

'Were you?' Taking a deep breath, Antonia halted and turned to face him. 'Why?'

His dark features were surprisingly sombre. 'Why do you think?'

'I really can't imagine.' Antonia tried to quell her rapidly accelerating heart. 'But I'd be glad if you could make it brief. I don't have a lot of time.'

'You do eat lunch, don't you?' he enquired tensely, the errant breeze lifting the collar of the black silk shirt

he was wearing. In an equally sombre black leather
jacket and black denims, he looked as disruptively
attractive as ever, and Antonia's eyes were unwillingly
drawn to the brown column of his throat rising from
the unbuttoned neckline. 'I was beginning to wonder.'

'What do you mean?' Dragging her eyes away,
Antonia endeavoured to maintain an offhand manner,
forcing herself to think of Celia, and what this might
mean to her.

'I mean I waited yesterday, without any success,' he
responded, glancing impatiently up and down the street.

Antonia's lips parted. 'You waited yesterday!' she
echoed.

'That's what I said,' he conceded drily.

She shook her head. 'I generally eat lunch in the
dining hall.'

'Really.' His tone was sardonic now, and he cast
another doubtful look around him. 'I should have
thought of that.'

Antonia strove to retain her indifference. 'I don't see
why,' she remarked, observing out of the corner of her
eye a traffic warden just turning the corner. 'Do you
know you're parked on yellow lines?'

'As I collected a couple of tickets yesterday, I
should,' he responded briefly. 'Antonia . . .'

'Then I should warn you, there's a traffic warden
coming this way,' she interrupted him crisply, closing
her ears to the explicit oath he uttered. 'I think you'd
better move your car, Mr Gallagher. Unless you enjoy
contributing to the Greater London authority.'

Reed's mouth compressed. 'Will you have lunch with
me?' he demanded, quickly measuring the distance
between himself, the traffic warden, and the car, but
Antonia had to refuse him.

'I can't,' she denied swiftly, already moving away
from him, and with a gesture of frustration, he turned
and strode back to the Lamborghini.

There was an arcade just a few yards further along
the street where Antonia generally did her shopping,
and resisting the impulse to look back and see whether

Reed had succeeded in his bid to avoid another fine, she
turned into the covered walkway. Her heart was still
beating much faster than it should, notwithstanding the
speed with which she had put some distance between
herself and temptation, and she stood for several
minutes looking into the window of a newsagent,
without actually seeing any of the display.

Why was he doing this? she asked herself over and
over. It didn't make sense. He had a beautiful fiancée,
who cared about him, and doubtless other opportunities
for diversion, should he so desire them, so why was he
picking on her? If he wanted sexual excitement, why
didn't he simply find another girl of his own kind to
feed his ego? A girl who would be flattered by his
attentions, and perfectly willing to keep their liaison a
secret. Or was it the fact that she was different, that she
came from a different sort of background, that
provided the stimulation, Antonia wondered. Perhaps
he thought she might be easier to cajole, or unlikely to
put up too much opposition, so long as she was
compensated in other ways. Like ... with a gift of
flowers, for example ...

The idea was so abhorrent to her, Antonia had
walked out of the arcade again and into the street
before she realised she had bought none of the things
she had come out for. She was trembling so badly, it
was almost an effort to put one foot in front of the
other, and she decided to abandon her expedition and
go back to work.

'Are you feeling all right?'

The kindly male voice startled her, and she swayed a
little unsteadily as an elderly gentleman touched her
arm. 'I ... oh ... yes, I'm fine,' she managed, hoping
he would not think her stricken expression was the
result of his considerate enquiry. Just for a moment, she
had thought it was Reed speaking to her, and she didn't
feel capable of coping with him right now.

'Are you sure?' The old gentleman was evidently
concerned about her, and Antonia struggled to reassure
him.

'I must be hungry,' she said, summoning a thin smile, and then her breath caught in her throat as she saw the lean dark figure making straight for them. She should have known Reed wouldn't give up that easily, she thought unsteadily, wondering if she dared ask the old man to protect her. But the circumstances were such, she could not involve anyone else.

Reed reached them seconds later, his keen grey eyes raking Antonia's face with growing concern. 'What's wrong?' he asked, his hand beneath her elbow that much more demanding than the older man's had been, and her erstwhile knight-errant turned to him with relief.

'Your young lady's feeling a little faint,' he declared, clearly identifying Reed as someone he could relinquish his responsibilities to. 'She says she's hungry. Perhaps you should see she gets something to eat right away.'

'I'll do that,' said Reed smoothly, the pressure of his fingers on her arm warning her not to contradict him. He looked down at her with apparent indulgence. 'Sorry I'm late, Antonia. I had some difficulty in parking the car.'

Antonia's jaw quivered with a mixture of impotence and frustration, but when Reed's fingers compelled her to move on, she had little choice but to go with him. She was not strong enough to fight with him, not right now, and besides, a weakening feeling of inertia was sweeping over her. She was tired, and hungry, and the effort of simply sparring with him had robbed her of most of her resistance.

'Why are you doing this?' she exclaimed wearily. 'You know someone might see us. And besides, doesn't it mean anything to you that I don't want to eat lunch with you?'

'If I thought that, I wouldn't be here,' Reed responded, with brutal arrogance. 'Now, I've parked the car in the carpark at the back of here. I suggest we go and find it and . . .'

'No!' With quivering determination, Antonia pulled herself away from him. 'No, I won't go with you!' She

shook her head. 'I don't know where you've got the
idea from that I might like to have lunch with you, but
it's mistaken, believe me! Now, please—go away and
stop bothering me!'

'*Antonia* . . .'

'Mrs Sheldon!'

'All right, Mrs Sheldon then.' His lips tightened with
the effort to be civil. 'Can you deny that you're in no fit
state to be left on your own . . .'

'Because of you!' she interrupted him unsteadily, and
he politely inclined his head.

'If you say so,' he conceded, neither denying nor
admitting the charge. 'Even so, I'd be one hell of a
bastard if I walked off and left you now. So I suggest
we find somewhere you can sit down, and I'll buy you a
drink or a sandwich or whatever it takes to put some
colour back into your face.'

Antonia took a deep breath. 'I'm not leaving here.'

'I'm not suggesting you should.' He glanced round.
'How about that pub over there? They're bound to
serve bar snacks at lunchtime. Let me buy you a drink
and a ham roll or something.' He paused. 'Just to prove
I'm not the villain you seem to think me.'

Antonia sighed. 'And if someone sees us?'

Reed's lips twisted. 'Are you ashamed of being seen
with me?'

'You *know* what I mean!'

'Someone *I* know?'

'Yes.'

'So what?' He shrugged. 'I'm only buying you a
drink. Where's the harm in that?'

Where indeed? Antonia pondered uneasily, reluctantly
following Reed into the bar of the pub. Except that she
should have been more positive, instead of giving in to
what could only be regarded as a reckless impulse.

The Black Lion turned out to be a favourite haunt of
students from the institute, Antonia discovered, and she
saw several familiar faces as she made her way to the
comparative anonymity of a corner booth. She hoped
no one recognised her. As yet, her features were not

well known outside Mr Fenwick's domain. But she had not taken into account the fact that as a newcomer she had inspired a great deal of interest among the male fraternity. Tall and slim, with the full breasts she so abhorred, she had attracted a considerable amount of admiration, and more than one of the trainees had expressed the aspiration to be the focus of her long, faintly Oriental eyes.

The booths were all occupied, but the one in the corner had two vacant seats on a banquette, facing a young couple who were evidently engrossed in one another. Antonia chose this, sliding on to the cool vinyl pad with some relief. In spite of her reluctance to spend any longer with Reed than was absolutely necessary, she was grateful for the chance to sit down and recover her self-possession. And surely now she had an opportunity to make him see he was wasting his time by pursuing her?

Reed had got their drinks, and she lifted her hand to let him see where she was. He came across carrying the two drinks in one hand and two ham and salad rolls in a paper napkin in the other. Setting the drinks on the table, he slid on to the banquette beside her, and although she had moved to the farthest extremities of the booth, his thigh brushed hers as he took his seat.

As usual, he looked perfectly at home in what must be, for him, unfamiliar surroundings. Swallowing a mouthful of the glass of lager he had bought for himself, he surveyed the busy environs of the bar with casual interest, apparently unaware that the girl opposite had transferred her attention from her boyfriend to him.

'What is this?' Antonia asked bleakly, to distract the girl's assessing gaze, and Reed turned his head to look at her. This close, the disruptive influence of his darkly fringed eyes was devastating, and forcing herself to concentrate on the glass in front of her, Antonia made her meaning plain.

'It's brandy,' Reed told her, putting down his glass and pushing hers towards her. 'Drink it. It will do you good. You look as though you need it.'

Aware that their conversation was being monitored by the young woman opposite, albeit that she had been obliged to return her attention to her boyfriend, Antonia felt her indignation rising. 'What do you mean by that?' she enquired, barely audibly, but Reed's expression revealed he had heard.

'Pale,' he said, lifting his hand and running his knuckles down her cheek, and although she flinched away from him, she could still feel his touch long after it had departed.

Deciding she needed the raw spirit after all, Antonia took a sip of the brandy, catching her breath as it forged its way down into her stomach. But he was right. It was warming. And she took another sip before examining her sandwich.

'They only had ham and salad,' Reed remarked, biting into the crisp roll he had bought for himself. 'I hope you like it.'

Antonia made no response, but she did nibble at her own sandwich, meeting the eyes of the young woman opposite with rather more confidence than before. After all, she could hardly blame her for looking at Reed, she thought. He was good to look at. And nor could she blame her if she was wondering what he was doing with someone like her.

'Is it okay?'

Reed emptied his mouth to take another drink of his beer, and Antonia nodded vigorously. 'Yes, thank you,' she answered politely, not responding to his evident desire for her to look at him, and he turned back to his roll with rigid application.

Antonia could not eat all her sandwich. It wasn't easy eating any of it with the twin disadvantages of Reed, and the girl opposite, observing her progress. But the brandy was soothing, and by the time her glass was empty, she was feeling more herself.

Reed, too, left half his roll, his appetite only lasting so long as Antonia was making an effort. However, without asking her permission he took their empty glasses back to the bar and returned with them filled,

his eyes challenging her to refuse him when his presence
on the banquette prevented her escape.

To Antonia's relief, the young couple opposite
departed a few moments later, and no one else came to
take their place. The crowd in the bar was thinning as
people made their way back to work, and glancing at
her watch, Antonia was horrified to discover it was
nearly half-past one.

'I should be leaving,' she said, taking a polite, if hasty
sip of her drink. 'Really, I'm due back in the office at a
quarter to two.'

'You'll be there,' stated Reed flatly, his gaze
flickering over her anxious face. 'There's no point in
asking you to take the afternoon off, is there? You're
honest and conscientious, as well as everything else.'

Antonia's breathing felt constricted. 'Mr Gallagher . . .'

'Reed.'

'*Mr Gallagher*, I think this conversation has gone far
enough.'

'Do you?' His lips curled in sudden mockery. 'Well,
yes, I guess you could be right. But that doesn't solve
my problem.'

'I don't think you have a problem, Mr Gallagher,'
Antonia retorted huskily. 'Please: I'd like to get out
now.'

'And if I don't let you?' he countered, his obstruction
causing her to meet his gaze.

'I could scream,' she retorted.

'Would you?' His eyes taunted her. 'Wouldn't that
just be doing what you're trying to avoid? Drawing
attention to us?'

'Please . . .'

'Say: *please, Reed*.'

Antonia closed her eyes against his unquestionable
attraction and repeated in a small, tense voice: 'Please,
Reed!'

'Okay.'

With a jack-knifing movement, he extricated himself
from the banquette, but when he would have given her

his hand to assist her, Antonia ignored it. Self-consciously aware that the heat of her body had practically glued her to the seat, she managed to lever herself out of the booth; marching stiffly ahead of him out of the pub.

Outside, she was almost amazed to discover the sun was still shining. The subdued lighting in the bar had given the impression that it was quite dull outside, and it was heartening to discover the day was still bright.

'I'll walk you back to the institute,' Reed said, when she would have nodded farewell and left him.

Antonia straightened her spine. 'That's not necessary.'

'I know it's not,' he responded tersely, falling into step beside her in spite of her denial. 'Tell me: what do you do at this institute? We've had lunch together, and I still know next to nothing about you.'

'I'm sure you wouldn't be interested,' replied Antonia annoyingly, and she sensed his controlled reaction.

'If I weren't, I shouldn't be asking,' he retorted, not quite succeeding in disguising his impatience. 'It's not a state secret, is it? You're not quietly a front for MI6?'

'Hardly.' Antonia felt an insurgent desire to laugh at the idea that Mr Fenwick might be involved in counter-espionage. Picturing the rotund director of the institute in the role of a latter-day James Bond didn't quite fit his image, and her lips twitched irresistibly at this portrayal of her employer. 'As a matter of fact, I work for the institute's director,' she volunteered now, deciding there was no harm in being honest with him. 'It's interesting work. I like it.'

Reed inclined his head. 'But you're not from London, are you?'

'No.' Antonia took a deep breath. 'Didn't your fiancée tell you?' she asked, introducing Celia's name deliberately. 'I come from the north of England; Newcastle, to be exact. I've only lived in London for the past two months.'

'And do you like it?' he asked, not taking her up on his fiancée's involvement, and she shrugged.

'I've told you. I like my work. For the rest—well, I miss my family.'

They had reached the institute now, and halting, she turned to say goodbye. 'Thank you for my lunch,' she said, as if she was reciting the words, and Reed thrust his hands into his trouser pockets, as if to prevent himself from actual physical violence.

'I want to see you again,' he said, stepping closer to her, and she could feel, as well as smell, the heat of his body. 'Now, don't give me any nonsense about its not being a good idea, or what will Celia say,' he added huskily. 'Just say yes, for once in your life, without weighing the pros and cons.'

'I can't . . .'

'Oh, for Christ's sake!'

'I can't,' she repeated unsteadily, stepping back from him. With the warmth and the musky male scent of him enveloping her, it was incredibly difficult to refuse him, but the sanity of reason eventually prevailed. 'Look,' she appended stiffly, 'I realise you're probably used to young women falling at your feet, but I can't help it. I have no intention of providing a novelty for you or anyone else, and if you want a *gutter* experience, I suggest you look elsewhere!'

CHAPTER FOUR

THE offices of the Gallagher Trust and Investment Corporation were in a quiet square, just off the Strand. When Reed's grandfather took over the company in 1920, its assets only ran to two floors of a rather seedy tenement building near King's Cross, but the old man had changed all that. With the first Great War behind them, people were eager to invest in anything which would bring them a swift profit, and Reed's grandfather had turned this to his advantage. While other speculators concentrated on the stock market, Declan Gallagher bought property, putting his client's money into solid bricks and mortar, that were still standing long after the crash of Wall Street had left less astute investors penniless.

The business grew and expanded, and in the 1950s Reed's father continued its advance, looking overseas for new avenues to explore. Now Gallaghers, as they were dubbed on the stock market, had shares in diamond mines in Africa, oil wells in Alaska, cattle ranches in South America; they owned an air charter company and a fleet of oil tankers; they farmed 10,000 acres of prime farmland in Somerset and Wiltshire, and their chemical laboratories had produced new and more sophisticated types of fertiliser to satisfy the standards of the stiffest conservationists. In fact, the Gallagher corporation was involved in most aspects of technological advancement, and its board of directors was a comprehensive mix of accountants, scientists, engineers, and statisticians—of which Reed classed himself among the latter.

Since his father's retirement at sixty, three years ago, Reed himself had become the board's chairman. He was young, only thirty when Joseph Gallagher adhered to his wife's advice to retire, while he was still young

49

enough to enjoy life. But in the past three years, Reed
had confirmed the confidence his father had had in him
and now, at thirty-three, there was little about the
company he did not know. He had always been
interested in maths and a degree in economics at
Oxford had reinforced his natural ability to understand
figures. In addition, he had spent at least part of each
year visiting the company's operations overseas, and
although he had learned how to delegate, his intimate
knowledge of each project made him a formidable
adversary.

Reed had always loved the company. As a schoolboy,
he had spent hours at the office during his holidays,
watching the computors, studying the telex machine, as
it rattled out its messages from all around the world. He
found finance an infinitely fascinating subject, not
simply in its capacity to make money, but rather as a
means to exercise his mental abilities. It was a challenge
to predict trends, to anticipate shortfalls, to try and
keep one step ahead of the stock market. Had he not
been able to step into his father's shoes, he assumed he
would have been an economist or a stockbroker, and
sometimes, like today, he wished he had had the choice.

Reed's office, the office his father and grandfather
had occupied before him, was on the penthouse floor of
the building, and overlooked the nearby recreation
ground. At this hour of a Friday afternoon, he could
see several joggers, doggedly marking the boundaries of
the play area, and gradually the swings and roundabouts
were set in motion, as children came from school to fill
them up.

Reed glanced impatiently at the narrow gold watch
on his wrist. What time was it? he wondered irritably,
his mouth compressing when he saw it was only half-
past four. Another hour-and-a-half before Celia had
said she would arrive, so that they could drive down to
Sussex together. Another ninety minutes before they set
away for the weekend with Celia's parents in the
country.

Reed expelled his breath heavily. He was not looking

forward to this weekend with the Lytton-Smythes. It wasn't their fault; it wasn't even Celia's fault. He was just out of sorts with himself, and the idea of a weekend spent being polite to Celia's parents filled him with depression.

Leaving the window, Reed walked back to his desk, idly flicking over the papers requiring his inspection. He had work he could do, but he was strangely lacking in application, and for the first time in his life he had no interest in whether the storms raging in northern Canada would delay their oil explorations another month, or if the overthrow of a certain central African dictator would facilitate their efforts to gain mining rights. He was bored and indifferent, the restless energy he usually poured into his business dealings lacking its normal direction.

There was no rational reason for his dissatisfaction, he acknowledged now, drumming his fingers on the tooled leather pad. There was no crisis in the company, no especial problem he had to deal with. Even his personal life was exactly as he had wished it. Celia was a beautiful girl, and their relationship was perfectly satisfactory. So what was wrong?

Thinking of Celia, he glanced again at his watch, but it was still only twenty-five minutes to five. Eighty-five minutes to take-off, he reflected broodingly, despising his introspection. Perhaps he needed a drink. Perhaps a small measure of alcohol would help to lift the demoralising cloud that was hovering over him.

Pouring himself a double whisky, he carried the glass back to his desk, and dropping down into his leather chair, he propped his feet on the desk. The alcohol felt good as it found its way down into his stomach, and he decided Ladbroke could drive them down to Five Oaks. He felt like getting drunk, and there was plenty of time before Celia would put in an appearance.

Celia . . .

Studying the spirit in his glass, Reed thought about his fiancée. He had known a lot of woman, before she came along—the natural result of being Joseph

Gallagher's son, he always assumed, his father's wealth overcoming a multitude of sins—but Celia was the first he had actually proposed to. She had seemed eminently fitted to being the wife of a man in his position, and as he was thirty-three, and his parents were eager for him to provide them with grandchildren, he had not objected to their active encouragement.

Besides, Celia was sweet; she flattered his ego; and if he occasionally found her conversation boring, it was no different from that of his friends' wives. He did not want to marry a businesswoman. He found women in the professions were more concerned with advancement than their male counterparts, and while he did not resent their ambition, he wanted a wife, not a business partner. So why was he so out of humour with himself? The answer was one he had avoided thus far. *Antonia Sheldon!*

There was no earthly reason why her behaviour towards him should have bothered him so much; but it did! Ever since Tuesday, he had been brooding over what had happened that lunchtime, and her ugly reaction to his friendly invitation had exposed a raw nerve.

Reed was not normally a violent man. On the contrary, he was known for his good humour, his charming personality, that successfully concealed a brain as acute as one of his own computers. On the whole he was an even-tempered man, used to disguising his innermost feelings, even in the face of extreme provocation. But Antonia Sheldon got beneath his skin; she had the uncanny ability to stir emotions he had not known he possessed, and it was disconcerting to realise that with her he could not always control his feelings.

He had wanted to follow her into that institute where she worked on Tuesday afternoon. The simmering rage which had gripped him at her insolent response had almost overwhelmed his natural discretion, and driving back to his apartment he had entertained himself with visions of her colleagues looking helplessly on, while his fingers round her throat squeezed the life out of her.

Since then, of course, he had endeavoured to put all thoughts of her out of his head, and to a certain extent, he had succeeded. The trouble was, he knew she was still there, whether consciously or subconsciously, and it was her image that was clouding his brain and blighting the coming weekend.

Finishing the whisky in his glass, he swung his feet abruptly to the floor and stood up. To hell with it, he thought savagely. He was going to see her one last time and tell her what he thought of her. Half his frustration came from knowing she thought she had had the last word. He would explain that her isolation had aroused his compassion; that he had felt *sorry* for her; that far from desiring her body, he had been trying to educate her mind, and if she had mistaken his—well meaning—invitation for something else, she had his sympathies.

Depositing the empty glass on his desk, he strode towards the heavy door which gave access to his secretary's office. 'I'm just going out for an hour, Mrs Drysdale,' he informed the efficient middle-aged woman, who had worked for his father before him. 'I should be back before six.'

'But—isn't Miss Lytton-Smythe expected?' Mrs Drysdale exclaimed in surprise, removing her horn-rimmed spectacles to look at him.

'Yes, she is,' Reed nodded, hardly pausing in his progress towards the outer door. 'But not before six, and as I've said, I'll be back by then. Relax, Mrs Drysdale. Everything's under control.'

'Did you sign those letters?'

Mrs Drysdale seemed loath to let him go, and Reed sighed, running a weary hand round the back of his neck. 'I've signed everything of importance,' he assured her crisply, impatient to be off. 'You can go, too, as soon as you're ready. Celia can find her own way into my office.'

'Yes, Mr Gallagher.'

Mrs Drysdale had no choice but to accept his edict, although Reed knew she, of all people, found it hardest to adapt to his ways. His father had always deferred to

her, as a matter of courtesy, but Reed was less in awe of
her admirable qualifications. In consequence, theirs was
a relationship based on tolerance, and there were times
he knew, as now, when she could not hide her
disapproval.

But Reed had no time at present to consider Mrs
Drysdale's feelings. He had exactly one hour to drive
across London, speak to Antonia, and drive back
again, and that, at the height of the Friday rush-hour,
was not going to be easy.

As luck would have it, he made good time to Clifton
Gate, and it was only just after a quarter-past-five when
he turned into the drive of Eaton Lodge. He knew,
from earlier enquiries he had made, that the institute
where Antonia worked closed at four-thirty on Fridays,
and even taking into account the vagaries of the buses,
she should be home by now.

Suppressing the instinct that what he was doing was
not only foolish but downright reckless, Reed crossed
the forecourt and entered the building. Antonia's door
was the first on the left, and without giving himself time
to have second thoughts, he knocked firmly on the
panels.

Infuriating though it was, as he stood there waiting
for her to open the door, a mental image of her pale
features suddenly flashed into his mind. As if he was
looking at a photograph, he could see every facet of her
indignant hazel eyes and stubborn mouth—the way she
had looked when he had last seen her. She had a nice
mouth, he reflected unwillingly, the lower lip fuller and
inclined towards sensuality—when she wasn't being
angry with him, of course. When she smiled, her whole
face lit up—a dazzling transformation—and her eyes
were not hazel then, but green . . .

'Are you looking for Mrs Sheldon?' enquired a
vaguely familiar voice behind him, and controlling his
impatience, Reed turned to face the caretaker's
inquisitive wife. 'Why—Mr Gallagher, it's you!' she
exclaimed, her thin features acquiring a decidedly
curious expression. 'Miss Lytton-Smythe's not here.'

'I know.' Reed pushed his thumbs into the pockets of his waistcoat, refusing to explain himself to her. 'I—it's Mrs Sheldon I wanted to see. Is she in?'

'Oh—she's gone!' declared Mrs Francis swiftly, and for a bone-jarring moment Reed thought she meant for good.

'Gone?' he echoed, his voice revealing a little of the emotion he was feeling, and Mrs Francis nodded.

'She was catching the six o'clock train,' she confided, folding her arms, as if preparing for a long intercourse. 'Gone home for the weekend, she has. You know: to Newcastle. Said she'd be back Sunday night, if that's any help to you.'

Reed withdrew his thumbs from his pockets, aware of a shuddering sense of relief sweeping over him at her words. It was a debilitating experience, and he could have done with a drink now to restore his equilibrium, but instead, he had to convince Mrs Francis that he was grateful for her assistance.

'Well—thank you,' he said, running his tongue over dry lips. 'It . . . wasn't important.'

'Would you like me to give her a message?' Mrs Francis persisted, clearly sensing some intrigue here and loath to let him go without an explanation. 'I'm sure she'll be sorry to have missed you. She doesn't get many visitors, you know.'

Reed's lips twisted a little in self-derision. He had few doubts that Antonia would welcome the omission, and far from being sorry to have missed him, she would resent his implicating her in what would seem a reckless indiscretion.

'As I say, it's not important, Mrs Francis,' he declared, moving firmly towards the outer door. 'I—I had a message for her from Celia. But as she's gone away, it doesn't matter.'

'Oh, I see.'

Mrs Francis accepted his account with an understanding smile, but Reed could still see the doubtful speculation in her eyes. What the hell was he going to tell Cee, he wondered savagely, nodding a farewell and striding back to his car. Now that Mrs Francis was involved, he was going to have to say something, and his brain buzzed frustratedly as he drove back to his office.

Mrs Lord had brought Susie to the station to meet the train. In spite of the lateness of the hour for her, she was jumping with excitement by the time her mother walked through the ticket barrier, and Antonia bent and gathered her small daughter into her arms.

'Hello, treasure,' she said emotively, burying her suddenly tear-wet face in the hollow of her daughter's shoulder. 'It's so good to be back! Have you been a good girl for Nanna?'

'She's been as good as gold since Tuesday,' declared Mrs Lord drily, returning her daughter's kiss and wiping a recalcitrant tear from Antonia's cheek. 'All I've heard is how many days it is to Friday, and what present might you have bought her for her birthday.'

Her mother's careless mention of Tuesday brought a momentary pang of conscience, but Antonia quickly dismissed it. She was not going to allow Reed Gallagher to spoil her weekend, she told herself fiercely, and concentrated her attention on Susie's description of her birthday cake.

'We're having a party,' she explained, holding tightly to her mother's hand as they walked to where Mrs Lord had left her car. 'Uncle Howard and Auntie Sylvia, and David and Kevin, are coming to tea tomorrow, and Nanna said I could ask three of my friends from school.'

'Super,' said Antonia affectionately, exchanging a wordless look of gratitude with her mother. 'Six seven-year-olds! That's all I need! I can see this is going to be a very restless couple of days.'

In fact, the weekend tended to drag. Even in so short a time, Antonia had lost touch with her mother's life in Gosforth, and although initially they had plenty to talk about, by Sunday there was a definite lack of communication.

On Friday evening, Susie had dominated the conversation, both while she was there and after she had gone to bed. Antonia had been relieved to see her daughter did not appear to have suffered any ill effects from her absence. Susie was just as ebullient as ever, and Antonia was more inclined to accept her mother's assertion of out of sight, out of mind.

Saturday morning started with Susie opening her presents. Antonia had brought her a doll that mimicked many of the actions of a real baby, but although Susie was intrigued by its ability to drink its bottle and wet its nappy, she spent more time playing with the electronic game her grandmother had provided.

'Children are notoriously fickle,' remarked Mrs Lord, as she and Antonia sat in the large, sunlit kitchen, lingering over their mid-morning cup of coffee. 'As soon as you've gone, she'll discover that she likes the doll best of all. You'll see. I'm usually right.'

As Susie disappeared into the garden to play soon afterwards, and her mother departed for a hair appointment, Antonia was left to mooch around the house for the rest of the morning. It was odd, she thought. When she was at the flat, she had longed to be at home, back among the people and the places she knew so well. But now she was here, she was restless. Even the surroundings of her old room, which her mother had never altered, in spite of her marriage to Simon, failed to give her the pleasure she had expected. She found herself missing the constant throb of traffic that it was never quite possible to block out of the apartment, the awareness of a city that never seemed to sleep.

Of course, she was being foolish; and she knew it. The persistent hum of traffic was one of the things she had found hardest to adjust to, and she certainly could not wish to duplicate it here in Gosforth. And as for thinking that London never slept: well, that was true of sections of every capital city and every smaller one, as well. Hospitals; law enforcement; public services; there was always someone working for the good of the community, at all hours of the day and night. There was nothing remarkable about that. She was being ridiculously fanciful in associating it only with London. For goodness sake, what was she thinking of? She had hated it to begin with.

Sitting on the edge of her bed, she drew up one slim leg and rested her chin on her knee. The trouble was, she admitted ruefully, she had been feeling pretty rotten since last Tuesday. No matter how she tried to justify her behaviour, she could not get past the fact that Reed had bought her lunch and she had paid him back by insulting him. Oh, she could find a dozen reasons to exonerate her rudeness—he had no right to send her flowers; he had been given no reason to presume on the flimsiest of introductions that she might be willing to have lunch with him, let alone dinner—but they did not ease her conscience. She had behaved like a timid virgin, embarking on her first date, instead of acting like the mature woman she was, and accepting his friendship in like manner. Men and women could have perfectly platonic relationships, she reminded herself irritably. He probably thought she was a prime example of a raw northern upbringing, a mixture of ignorance and prudery, stodginess and unsophistication.

Antonia's brother and his wife arrived in the afternoon, and the tea-party that followed left little time for conversation or introspection. Howard's twins left a trail of havoc wherever they went, and what with mopping up orange juice and scooping jelly off her mother's carpet, Antonia felt physically exhausted by the time they all went home.

Sylvia, her sister-in-law, did find an opportunity while they were washing up to ask her if she was enjoying working in London. 'I envy you, I do honestly,' Howard's wife averred fiercely. 'I wish I had a reason to dump my kids on your mother and clear off to pastures new! Sometimes I think I'll go mad if Howard doesn't find a way to discipline our Kevin!'

'He's only a boy,' said Antonia reassuringly, even though she didn't like Sylvia's dig about *dumping* Susie.

'I expect he'll quieten down as he gets older. Howard was quite a handful, I believe, when he was that age.'

'Really?' Sylvia grimaced. 'Well, that's not what he says. He blames our family for Kevin's unruly streak. I told him—I said, there's no one in our family who behaves like a hooligan every time we're in company. But he doesn't listen. He really gets me mad!'

Deciding this conversation was moving into areas she didn't have any right to enter, Antonia changed the subject. 'I like your dress,' she said generously, admiring Sylvia's plaid smock. 'Is it new? It suits you.'

'I got it in town,' Sylvia replied without enthusiasm. 'I suppose you got that dress in London. You can always tell.'

As Antonia was wearing the cream shirt-waister she had worn to Celia's party, she smiled. 'As a matter of fact, I bought this in the sales last January,' she answered, thrusting back the memories it insistently evoked. 'Sorry to disappoint you, Sylvia, but I haven't bought any clothes since I went to London. I don't need any and, even if I did, I can't afford them.'

Sunday was the worst day of all. Although Antonia knew she would not want to leave when it was time to do so, the morning seemed endless. Her mother, as always, went to church, taking Susie with her. Antonia should have accompanied them, she knew, but in spite of her mother's admonishments, she did not feel up to one of the Reverend Lisle's sermons. Besides, someone had to prepare the Sunday dinner, she said, as they were having it in the middle of the day, even though peeling potatoes and cutting up the other vegetables did not take more than half an hour.

During the afternoon, Antonia packed her bag again, and ordered a taxi to take her to the station to catch the five o'clock train. 'I'd rather you didn't come with me, Mum,' she told her mother gently. 'It will be easier for Susie if she doesn't have to wave me goodbye on the platform. This way, it won't seem so terrible when I've gone.'

Susie, however, saw things differently. 'I want to

come to the station,' she wailed, her face crumpling up
when she saw her mother's case in the hall. 'I like going
to the station. I like seeing all the trains.'

'There aren't that many trains on a Sunday,' Antonia
comforted her unhappily, pulling the little girl on to her
lap. 'Oh, don't cry, darling. You know Mummy's got to
go back.'

'When can I come to London?' Susie persisted, her
lower lip trembling. 'I want to see where you live. You
said I could come to the flat.'

'Next holidays,' promised Antonia rashly, exchanging
a helpless look with her mother. 'Nanna will bring you
down in about a month. You can both stay for a long
weekend, and I'll show you the Houses of Parliament
and Buckingham Palace, where the Queen lives.'

'Really?' Susie stuck her thumb in her mouth and
regarded her mother doubtfully.

'Yes, really,' said Antonia, removing Susie's thumb
with a reproving frown. 'So—how about helping me
make a sandwich to eat on the train? I shan't be able
to stay for tea, and there are no buffet cars on
Sundays.'

Later, as the train pulled out of Newcastle station,
Antonia had to steel herself not to shed a few tears. But
they were not really for Susie, they were more for
herself, she reflected ruefully. Susie had her grandmother
to turn to; she felt as if she had no one.

It was almost ten o'clock when the train pulled into
King's Cross station. The journey, which generally took
a little over three hours, had lengthened to nearly five,
due to repairs being made to the line at Peterborough.
Half-empty, the train had chugged its way through a
series of rural stations, stopping at every one, and those
passengers who were not reading had fallen asleep out
of boredom.

Unfortunately, Antonia had neither the will to read
nor the relaxation necessary to go to sleep, and by the
time the train reached London, she felt utterly
miserable. The flat, which had not seemed so bad from
a distance, had lost its appeal by the mile, and she

tugged her case down from the rack, wishing for once she had chosen to share an apartment with another girl.

Even Celia Lytton-Smythe shared with Liz Ashford, she reflected, unwillingly thinking of her glamorous neighbours. She wondered what they had been doing this weekend. Not spending five unproductive hours on a draughty train, she was sure. People like Celia and Liz—and Reed, too, she assumed, although she knew nothing about him—went everywhere by car or by plane. They did not waste their time on journeys that could comfortably be avoided.

As soon as the train had stopped, Antonia got out, tugging her suitcase after her. It was not heavy. She had not taken much home with her. But it was cumbersome, and it knocked against her legs as she struggled along the platform.

A collector was waiting to take their tickets as they passed through the barrier. Antonia handed hers over, and then set her suitcase on the ground to loop the strap of her bag over one shoulder, and switch the heavier item to her other hand.

As she did so, she got the distinct impression that someone was watching her, and she looked up in dismay, hoping she was not going to have to fend off some unwanted admirer. After the strain of the last five hours, she felt too weary to be polite, and the first twinges of a headache were probing at her temples.

'Reed!'

Her involuntary use of his name was instinctive. It was the way she had been thinking of him for the past two weeks, if she was honest, and the idea of addressing him as *Mr* Gallagher was far from her thoughts at that moment.

Reed was waiting for her. From his stance, she suspected he had been there for some time, which seemed to be confirmed by the way he came stiffly to meet her. He was unsmiling, his dark features drawn into an enigmatic mask, but he bent and took her case from her, and she was too shocked to prevent him.

CHAPTER FIVE

Antonia pulled herself together and hastened after him, noticing inconsequently how well the brown leather jacket sat upon his shoulders. Beneath was a fine wool sweater, also in shades of brown and gold, and a pair of narrow Levis completed his attire. She didn't think of arguing with him; not at that moment. Just finding him here, waiting for her, seemed the most natural thing in the world, and she would have plenty of time later to question her judgment.

Reed deposited her suitcase in the boot of the car and then unlocked the doors. 'Get in,' he said, swinging open the one on the nearside, and Antonia complied, glad she was wearing her corded trouser suit.

The door was closed and Reed walked round the bonnet to get in beside her. Between them, the gear console prevented any accidental contact, but he did not immediately start the car; instead, he half-turned in his seat towards her.

'The train was late,' he observed, his features vaguely discernible in the light cast from the station. 'I enquired, and they said they expected it in at nine.'

'Yes.' Antonia endeavoured to sound as composed as he did. 'There was a diversion. Some repairs being done to the line, they said. I'm sorry. H-have you been waiting long?'

'Since nine o'clock,' he conceded expressionlessly. 'You don't seem surprised to see me.'

'Oh, I am.' Antonia shook her head. 'It's just—well, you're here, and ... and I'm grateful. I was feeling pretty awful when I got off the train.'

'And now?'

'And now——' His eyes looked black in the shadows and she lifted her shoulders helplessly. 'I—I'm glad you came,' she mumbled, turning her face away from him. 'I

63

wanted to apologise anyway. For . . . for what I said on Tuesday.'

'Did you?' She heard his sharp intake of breath at her words. 'Yes—well, you might not have felt that way if you had been at home on Friday afternoon.'

'What do you mean?'

Antonia's hair swung forward as she looked at him, half-concealing her expression behind its silky curtain, and Reed's cold fingers looped it back behind her ear. 'I came round to the flat to verbally tear you to pieces,' he confided with asperity, his hand lingering rather longer than was necessary beneath her ear-lobe. 'Unfortunately, Mrs Francis intercepted me to tell me you were away for the weekend, and I had to invent some asinine story about my delivering a message to you, from Cee.'

Antonia went suddenly still. 'So—so that's why you're here,' she said, all the warmth leaving her voice as things swung sickeningly back into perspective. He had not come to meet her because he wanted to. He had come because he dare not allow her to contradict anything Mrs Francis might say to her.

With a sob rising in her throat, she reached impulsively for the door handle. She didn't need a personal warning. A simple telephone call would have sufficed. She had no wish to hurt Celia, any more than he evidently did, and she wanted to get out of this car and away from him before she made an even bigger fool of herself.

'You're crazy!' Reed's voice behind her was rough with emotion, and there was a rattle of keys as he switched off the ignition without starting the engine. 'Do you really think I'd stand here in the cold for over two hours, just to get you to cover my story?' he demanded, his hard fingers digging into her shoulders, as he compelled her round to face him. 'Oh, Antonia— you don't know me very well yet, do you? But you're going to! Believe me, you're going to!'

'You . . . you said you'd been waiting since nine o'clock,' she protested, her hands against the fine cashmere sweater providing a barrier between them, and Reed sighed.

'I have,' he responded huskily, and in spite of her efforts his lips brushed her temple. 'I didn't say I'd been waiting *only* since nine o'clock,' he amended. 'I've been here since about seven-thirty, I suppose. I didn't know what train you were likely to get, so I compromised.'

Antonia shook her head. 'But you ... you said you were mad with me,' she exclaimed, as his sensuous mouth touched her cheek, and his warm breath was expelled in a rush of wry amusement.

'I was,' he said evenly. 'But that was on Friday. Since then, I've had a change of heart. Not least because of the shock I got when that old busybody told me you had gone.'

'Mrs Francis,' said Antonia flatly, as Reed's tongue stroked her skin, and he nodded.

'The same,' he agreed, his lips hovering near her mouth, and she abruptly turned her head aside to avoid the inevitable consequence.

'Are you going to take me home?'

'Eventually,' he conceded, accepting the rebuff and removing his hands. 'But first, we'll have some supper. You look half-starved, as well as half-frozen.'

'I don't think we should,' she declared as he turned back to the wheel, and he paused to give her a weary look.

'Well, that's par for the course, I suppose,' he responded cynically, starting the engine. 'But now you've made the statutory protest, can we enjoy what's left of the evening? You're going to have supper with me. Accept it. Call it ... compensation, if you like, for my perseverance.'

All the way along Euston Road and on down Portland Place into Regent Street, Antonia kept telling herself that she ought to be more forceful. She should demand that Reed take her home this instant, or set her down so that she could catch the bus. It was foolish to pretend he was just being friendly. Friends did not indulge in the kind of interplay Reed had indulged in at the station, and she had no way of knowing what manner of man he was. He could be a sex maniac, for all she knew. Just because he treated Celia with respect, did not mean he treated all women the same. And if she disappeared right now, who would know where she had gone? She'd be just another missing person, one of the hundreds who disappeared in London every year.

She shook her head frustratedly, and saw that they had turned into St James's Street. She didn't honestly believe Reed was dangerous—at least, not in a violent way. But what they were doing was wrong, both ethically and morally, and she was to blame for allowing it to go on.

The sudden descent into a darkened cavern was startling enough to drive all other thoughts out of her head. One minute, they were above ground, and the next the car had thudded over a ramp and swooped down into the bowels of the earth.

The realisation that it was an underground carpark gave her some relief, but the polite acknowledgment of the carpark attendant rekindled her anxieties. Where were they? she wondered, looking doubtfully at Reed's dark profile, and his lips parted in satisfaction as he drew into an empty space.

'Okay. Let's go,' he said, switching off the engine, and thrusting open his door, and Antonia gazed up at him in surprise.

'Go?' she echoed. 'Go where?'

'To have supper, of course,' he said resignedly, walking round the car to open her door. 'Come on. You don't want to create a scene, do you? Harry knows me quite well, and I wouldn't want to upset him.'

Antonia hesitated. 'Mr Gallagher——'

'It's Reed,' he said flatly, his hand beneath her elbow practically lifting her out of her seat. 'And you used it earlier, before you remembered it was *verboten*!'

She let him help her out, partly because she was convinced he would break her arm if she didn't, and partly because, as he had said, Harry was watching them.

'You hurt my arm,' she told him stiffly, as he locked the car, and he permitted her a brief appraisal.

'I'll massage it for you,' he said, his hand in the small
of her back directing her towards a bank of lifts, that
evidently gave access to the upper floors. 'Stop
worrying, can't you? I'm not taking you to a torture
chamber!'

Inside the lift, Antonia stood as far away from him as
she could, hoping it would stop and other people get in.
But he had used a key beside the button which
designated the twenty-second floor, and the lift
ascended swiftly, leaving her stomach far behind. She
assumed, as the twenty-second floor was the penthouse,
he was taking her to a rooftop restaurant, but when the
doors glided open, only a carpeted hallway and white-
panelled door confronted her.

'Out,' said Reed brusquely, compelling her to move
forward, and the lift closed behind them as he drew out
his keys again.

'Is this—is this . . .?'

'. . . my apartment,' agreed Reed drily, inserting a
perforated metal strip below the door handle. There
was a momentary pause as the computed key slid into
its compartment and then the door swung open. Reed
rescued the key again before urging Antonia ahead of
him, and although she was indignant, curiosity got the
better of her.

The first thing that caught her eyes in the subdued
lighting of the entrance hall was the magnificent
chandelier suspended overhead. It was not lit. Such
illumination as there was, was concealed above the
frieze that decorated the walls. But the prisms swung
together delicately, like wind chimes, in the sudden
draught from outside, drawing Antonia's attention and
inspiring her admiration.

She had little time to observe the other appointments
of the hall, however. The glossy darkwood table and the
antique mirror above received only the briefest of
appraisals, before Reed was impelling her past several
other doors to the one furthest away from the entrance.
The thick beige carpet, which had cushioned her feet in
the hall, flowed on into a room already illuminated by a

handful of lamps. The enormous, gold-coloured velvet sofas that met her bemused gaze provided oases of comfort in a room seemingly designed for that purpose. Everything in the room spoke of style and good taste, from the bowl of amber lilies occupying a low revolving bookcase, to the exquisitely laid-out chessboard, with its ebony and ivory pieces. The room was spacious, but its size had been tempered by the way the furniture was grouped, creating areas for reading or relaxing, or perhaps to listen to the elegant hi-fi system, cleverly concealed in a mahogany console. One wall was given over to bookcases, carelessly stacked alongside paperbacks and magazines; another comprised shelves of smoked glass, set with an interesting selection of sculptures, that invited a visitor's inspection; and finally the wall opposite was composed of windows, running from floor to ceiling, fluted by long blinds, and flanked by heavy cream velvet curtains.

'Hungry?' inquired Reed softly, lifting the jacket of her suit from her shoulders, and Antonia turned to him bewilderedly.

'This . . . is yours?' she asked faintly. 'You . . . *live* . . . here?'

'When I'm in town,' amended Reed evenly, depositing her jacket on the back of a chair and removing his own. 'I asked if you were hungry. Maria will have left us a snack in the dining room.'

Antonia swallowed. 'Maria?'

'My housekeeper,' Reed informed her tolerantly, loosening his tie. 'Come on. Let's go and see what she's left us. I don't know about you, but I could do with a drink.'

Antonia moistened her dry lips. 'Wh-where do you live when you're not in town?' she ventured, still overawed by her surroundings, and Reed sighed.

'I have a house in Oxfordshire. I'll show you that another day,' he promised, touching her shoulder. 'Now—do we eat, or do I satisfy my other instincts?'

She could feel the strength of his fingers, through the thin material of her blouse, and she moved swiftly out of reach. 'Wh-where is the dining room?' she asked, wondering how she had ever got herself into this position, and with a whimsical smile, he led the way across the living room and through a door that was hidden in the smoky recesses of the shelves.

Like the living room, the dining room had long windows overlooking the lights of London below. But the other walls were panelled here, surrounding a gleaming refectory table, capable of accommodating at least twenty people, with matching cushioned chairs upholstered in shades of green.

The 'snack' Reed had referred to, was laid out at one end of the table: a remarkable repast of smoked salmon and salad, rolls of ham stuffed with pineapple and skewered with olives, dishes of various kinds of fondue, with sticks of cheese and celery for dipping, and luscious black caviar, nestling on a bed of lettuce. There were sweet things, too: a meringue gâteau, two different types of cheesecake, and a fragrant dish of fruit salad, filled with every kind of fresh fruit imaginable, and flavoured with a trace of kirsch.

'Help yourself,' advised Reed easily, lifting a bottle of champagne out of its refrigerated bucket and expertly extracting the cork. The chilled liquid tumbled invitingly into long-stemmed glasses, and Reed handed one to her when she hesitantly looked his way. 'To us,' he said softly, touching his glass to hers, and she had swallowed a mouthful obediently before she realised what she was toasting.

'So . . .' Reed put down his glass again and regarded her gently. 'What would you like? As you're apparently not prepared to help yourself, I'll have to serve you.' He scooped a spoonful of caviare on to a round wafer and held it to her lips. 'Come on: taste it. It's delicious. Then you can tell me what you prefer.'

Antonia withstood his offering for only a moment before her lips parted. Reed studied her unknowingly provocative mouth for several seconds before popping the wafer inside, and Antonia's heart was pounding when he turned back to the table.

The caviare was nice, rather salty and distinctively flavoured. The champagne was good, too, much better than the rather indifferent sparkling wine she had had at her wedding. But every new experience underlined the vast gulf that stretched between Reed and herself, a gulf even she had not fully appreciated until tonight.

'Try the smoked salmon,' he suggested now, forking another small morsel for her delectation. 'Like it?' he asked lazily, his eyes on her mouth, and her knees felt suddenly weak and incapable of supporting her.

'I ought to go,' she got out carefully, putting down her glass. 'Really—I'm not awfully hungry, and it's getting very late.'

'It's barely eleven o'clock,' declared Reed persuasively, glancing at his watch.

'But I have to go to work tomorrow,' Antonia persisted.

'So do I.'

She shook her head. '*Do* you have a job?'

'You'd better believe it.' Reed was smilingly indignant. 'I'm not a playboy, if that's what you think.'

Antonia took a deep breath. 'Nevertheless . . .'

'Nevertheless—what?' Reed abandoned his attempt to tempt her with the food and came unnervingly towards her. 'Let's take our glasses and go back into the living room. We'll have another drink, and then I'll take you home.'

'Will you?'

Antonia looked at him doubtfully, and his expression sobered. 'If that's what you want,' he agreed, picking up his glass and the opened bottle of champagne and propping the door open with his shoulder. 'Come on. Maria will deal with that tomorrow.'

'Wh-where is Maria?' Antonia asked, glad of the diversion as she walked past him. Her shoulder brushed the wool of his sweater, and she was intensely conscious of the muscled frame beneath.

'I imagine she's in bed,' Reed replied, allowing the door to swing closed behind him. 'She generally retires soon after ten o'clock, I believe. I think she reads in bed.' He grinned suddenly. 'She devours romantic novels.'

Antonia bit her lip. 'You mean—she lives here, too?'

'Her rooms are on the other side of the kitchen,' explained Reed tolerantly. 'She has her own self-contained apartment, with her own lift. She likes it.' He nodded to the nearest sofa. 'Why don't you sit down?'

'Is—is she young—old—what?' asked Antonia, seating herself on the very edge of the sofa, her glass cradled protectively in her hand.

'She's a fifty-five-year-old German lady, who came to Ireland just after the war as an *au pair*, and has never wanted to go back,' declared Reed, setting the champagne bottle on the carved end table, and reclining on the cushions beside her. 'And that's the last word I'm going to say about Maria Mueller, is that clear? I didn't bring you here to conduct a discussion about my housekeeper's undoubted attributes!'

Antonia pressed her lips together. 'Why—why did you bring me here?'

Reed groaned. 'You know why. To have supper.'

'And that's all?' Antonia looked at him out of the corners of her eyes.

Reed turned his head against the honey-gold velvet. 'That's up to you.'

'What do you mean?'

'What do you think I mean?' he demanded, a trace of impatience colouring his tone. Pushing himself up he deposited his glass on the table beside the champagne bottle. 'For God's sake, stop looking at me like I was about to jump on you! I won't.' He paused, and when next he spoke his voice had thickened: 'Not unless you want me to, of course.'

Antonia was never sure whether it was the champagne on an empty stomach or some malicious demon inside her that inspired her next question, but the words were uttered, and she could not take them back: 'Do you want to?'

'Yes,' he said honestly, the fringe of dark lashes giving his face an oddly vulnerable expression, and

when a mutual feeling stirred inside her, Antonia
sprang abruptly to her feet.

'*You're* crazy!' she exclaimed, throwing his earlier
words back at him, but when his hand came up and
removed her glass, and then took her fingers to his lips,
she could not deny the aching sensation that ran down
her back and into her thighs.

'Sit down,' he said, tugging at her arm, and because
her legs were so unsteady, she complied. She came
down on to the sofa heavily, rocking the cushions, and
her breath caught constrictedly when she saw his lazy
smile.

'What are you trying to do? Break my sofa?' he
enquired with some amusement, trying to put her at her
ease. But the unconscious sensuality of her wide wary
eyes and parted mouth dispelled his humour, and his
hand slid behind her nape to massage the sensitive skin.

'I feel such a fool,' she breathed, realising the hem of
her blouse had separated from the waistband of her
trousers and trying unsuccessfully to restore it.

'You don't look a fool,' Reed assured her, using his
free hand to still her restless fingers and drawing them
instead to his lips again. Taking them into his mouth,
one by one, he caressed their sensitive pads with his
tongue, evoking sensations inside her Antonia knew she
had never experienced before.

'Reed, be sensible,' she whispered, prepared to make
one final protest, but his finger against her lips silenced
her.

'You're sensible enough for both of us,' he
responded, bearing her back against the soft cushions,
and then the hard beauty of his mouth found hers.

She had guessed he would be as good at this as he
was at getting his own way, but nothing had prepared
her for her own response. It was as if she had never
been kissed before, and certainly Simon, at his most
passionate, had never disturbed her as Reed was
disturbing her now. The probing pressure of his lips, the
sensuous invasion of his tongue, the possessive strength
of his hand behind her head, holding her imprisoned in

his grasp—he was arousing emotions she had hardly known existed, and although she was a mature woman, a *divorcee* moreover, she felt like an amateur in the hands of a professional.

Reed shifted, so the muscled weight of his body was lying half-over her, pressing her down into the cushions of the sofa. She could feel the sensuous brush of velvet at her back, where the gap her blouse had made exposed her bare midriff, and the powerful hardness of his legs against hers. His shirt was loose at the throat, and her hands moved compulsively to touch the brown skin rising above his collar. Her fingers curled instinctively into the silky hair at the back of his head, enjoying the unfamiliar intimacy, and he made a sound of pleasure as she caressed his neck.

She didn't understand it. Simon had kissed her; Simon had made love to her; they had even had a daughter together. Yet, she knew now, Simon had scarcely touched her deepest feelings: His fumbling overtures had often left her cold, and impatient for it to be over, and it dawned on her, with increasing certainty that what she had regarded as her own inadequacy had, in fact, been his. And had it not been for Susie, she might never have married him . . .

The sudden recollection of her daughter's existence was sobering. No matter how attractive the proposition, Reed's intentions were no different from what Simon's had been, and what he was doing was, if anything, more dangerous. With Simon, it had been bravado on her part, a need to prove she was as liberated as the next girl—a foolish contention, and one she had learned to regret. With Reed it was different. She wasn't a girl any longer; she was a woman, with a woman's needs, needs Simon had aroused, and just occasionally satisfied. Now, as Reed continued to kiss her, his lips finding the palpitating pulse at her temple, his tongue stroking the delicate contours of her ear, she was reminded of those needs, and alerted to an awareness of how pleasurable it would be to allow him to fulfil them. She would like to sleep with Reed, she realised guiltily; she would like to feel his skin against hers, without the cumbersome barrier of their clothes. And that was exactly why she had to get away from him, she acknowledged. It was years since she had taken a pill or used any other means to protect herself. At least Simon had wanted to marry her. Reed only wanted a diversion.

'No!' she said fiercely, as his hand slid down from her shoulder to touch her breast. His thumb, moving lazily over the swollen nipple already surging against the thin acrylic fibre of her blouse, halted its sensuous exploration, but his eyes were frankly disbelieving when he drew back a space to look down at her.

'No?'

'No,' she repeated huskily, pushing his hand away. 'Reed, I want to go home.'

He drew a deep breath and gently smoothed back the slightly damp hair at her temples. 'You *want* me,' he contradicted her softly, bestowing a disturbing kiss at the corner of her mouth. 'Just as much as I want you. Don't tell me no. I don't believe it.'

Antonia sighed. 'All right, all right,' she said, her body trembling. 'I—I do want you, but—but not on your terms.'

Reed's grey eyes narrowed. 'And what terms are they?' he asked quietly.

'Like—like this,' she stammered, her tongue circling her lips. 'At—at this time of night. Behind your fiancée's back!'

Reed drew back to support himself with a hand at either side of her. 'Might I remind you that you dictated the time,' he remarked narrowly. His lips tightened. 'And as for Cee—what she doesn't know can't hurt her!'

Antonia shrank from his words. 'And that's all that matters? That Celia shouldn't get to know about it?' she demanded contemptuously.

'No.' His cheeks hollowed. 'I'm not saying it's right——'

'What are you saying then?' She wriggled up against the cushions until her eyes were on a level with his. 'That you can't help yourself?'

'Something like that,' he retorted, astounding her. Then he turned abruptly away. 'Okay, okay. I'll take you home. Just give me a minute to—well, to control my baser instincts.'

Antonia hesitated, and then swung her legs to the floor and sat up beside him. She gave him a doubtful look. 'Are you all right?'

'Oh, fine!' Reed gave a short mirthless laugh.

Antonia shook her head. 'You don't understand.'

'I think I do.'

'I'm not a tease.'

'Did I say you were?'

'No, but——' She bent her head. 'You implied it. I can't help it if I'm not like the other women you deal with . . .'

'Wait!' Reed's harsh ejaculation interrupted her. '*What* other women?'

'Well, I assumed . . .'

'You assumed wrong then, didn't you?' Reed countered grimly, getting abruptly to his feet. 'Whatever opinion you have of my treatment of Cee, I *am not* in the habit of making clandestine assignations with other members of her sex. Oh, I admit I've been tempted, but contrary to your beliefs, I have respected my commitments. Until now.'

Antonia stood up also. 'Then—why? Why me?' she asked huskily, her expression revealing her confusion, and Reed's face hardened.

'I've been asking myself that for the past two weeks,' he responded, reaching for his jacket and putting it on. 'Come on.' He tossed her her jacket and turned towards the door. 'Let's go. Before I change my mind and decide to show you you're not as strongwilled as you like to think!'

The journey down in the lift was almost as traumatic as the journey up had been. Antonia kept her eyes averted from his lean intelligent face, knowing that if she looked at him, she might betray her feelings. She was frightened of the power he had over her, the ability he had to arouse her emotions and tug at her heart. He had been so right; she did *want* him, badly, and it was going to be *hell* to try and put him out of her mind.

The Lamborghini soon ate up the distance between Reed's home and the Victorian apartment building she lived in. It was nearly midnight, and the city streets were not busy, even if they were not exactly deserted. Reed drove smoothly, concentrating on the traffic there was, taking evasive action when a driver with probably an over-indulgence of alcohol in his veins swung wildly out of a side-street, and reverting to a crawl when a party of late-night revellers stepped incautiously out in front of him.

Antonia thought he would drop her at the gate, and her hand went out protestingly when he began to turn into the drive of Eaton Lodge. 'Don't,' she said, looking anxiously at his profile. 'Someone might recognise the car. It is rather—recognisable, isn't it?'

'You can't walk up there alone at this time of night,' said Reed doggedly, and Antonia sighed.

'Walk with me then,' she invited softly. 'Though I hardly think anyone is likely to attack me.'

Reed made no response to this. He merely gave her an enigmatic look before getting out of the car, and by the time he had rescued her case from the boot, Antonia was standing beside him.

In actual fact, she was glad he had decided to escort her up the drive. The privet hedge and the shrubs that were banked on either side were a little eerie in the darkness, and at this time of night the area was blanketed in silence. The outer door, which often stood open in daylight, was closed, and Antonia had to find her key to open it. Then, she turned to take her case from Reed.

'I—thanks,' she murmured, reaching out her hand, and he set the bulky suitcase down beside her.

'My pleasure,' he responded tautly, his features vaguely discernible in the half-light from the street lamp a few yards away.

'It—it's goodbye then,' she stammered, wishing he would go, and he nodded.

'Good*night*,' he amended, watching her changing expression. Then, with a groan of impatience, he bent his head. 'I'll call you,' he said, his mouth finding her parted lips with devastating intimacy. 'Sleep—if you can.' His lips twisted. 'I won't!'

CHAPTER SIX

'*Reed!* Are you listening to me?'

He turned, as the petulant tone of his fiancée's voice became a little shrill. 'Yes, I'm listening,' he assured her equably, moving away from his office window and resuming his seat behind his desk. 'You were saying Claire can't go to Paris, because she's discovered she's going to have a baby.'

'*Well!* You might show a little sympathy,' exclaimed Celia grumpily. 'I mean—what is she *doing*, getting herself pregnant! It's not as if *Paul* wants to marry her. He's far too happy running that club of his, to want to settle down to being a *father*!'

'Do you know that?' inquired Reed drily, trying to take an interest in the conversation. 'Aren't you forgetting Claire's a bright, intelligent woman? Paul may be flattered that she wants to marry him.'

'Oh, I don't know that she does,' retorted Celia restlessly, getting up from her chair and pacing about the room. 'She told me she's quite prepared to become a *single* parent. I mean, I ask you: what are her parents going to say about that!'

Reed shrugged, looking down at his fingers playing idly with his pen. 'I doubt if you'd be feeling so concerned if Claire was not letting you down, too,' he remarked flatly, his interest waning. 'Send someone else to Paris. What about Liz?'

Celia came back to the desk and rested her scarlet-tipped fingers on its surface. 'Liz won't go,' she declared ruefully. 'You know she hates flying, and going on her own ... No, she's out of the question.'

'So—what's the alternative?' Reed looked up at her.

Celia grimaced. 'I go myself, I suppose.'

Reed shrugged. 'Problem solved.'

'No, it's not.' Celia's lower lip jutted. 'Will you come with me?'

'No.' Reed's response was final. 'I've already told you——'

'I know, I know. You're going down to Stonor this weekend. But *couldn't* you change your mind?'

'Celia——'

'Oh, all right.' His fiancée lifted her hands from the desk and turned their palms towards him in a gesture of submission. 'I know you don't like fashion shows. But really, someone has to go, and I'm afraid it's going to have to be me.'

'As I said—problem solved.' Reed lay back in his chair and regarded her through his lashes. 'No sweat. I can go to Stonor on my own.'

Celia pursed her lips. 'I was looking forward to it; us being alone for two whole days!'

'Yes.' Reed averted his eyes. 'So was I. But there'll be other weekends.'

'Yes, there will, won't there?' Celia's smile appeared. 'After we're married, I expect we'll spend lots of weekends there.'

'After we're married, we'll be living there,' Reed reminded her tersely. 'Or had you forgotten?'

Celia wrinkled her nose. 'Well—not *all* the time, darling.'

'Stonor's near enough to London to commute,' Reed pointed out evenly. 'And I don't want my children growing up in this polluted atmosphere.'

'Your *children*! Darling, aren't you being just the teeniest bit premature?' Celia uttered a light laugh. 'Honestly, the way you talk, you'd think I was going to spend all my time *breeding*!'

Reed arched his dark brows. 'I did tell you I wanted a family, Cee.'

'I know you did.' Celia shifted beneath his steady gaze. 'But not straight away, surely? We need some time to ourselves.'

'If you say so.' Reed lifted his shoulders. 'We'll wait a year.'

'A *year*!' Celia sounded appalled. 'I thought—five years, at least.'

'That's too long.'

'We'll compromise.' Celia was eager to dismiss the subject. 'Besides, there's absolutely no need to condemn oneself to a rural existence, just because one has a family!'

'I don't want any child of mine left for days on end in the hands of a nursemaid,' retorted Reed curtly, aware that he was being unreasonable, but unable to prevent himself. 'When are you leaving?'

Celia looked sulky. 'Is that all you have to say? You pick an argument at the most inopportune time, and then ask me when I'm leaving, as if my feelings don't matter!'

Reed put down the pen before it snapped between his fingers, and looked up at her again. What a bastard he was, he thought, noticing the tremulous vulnerability of her mouth and the suspicious brightness of her eyes. Dear God, what was happening to him? This was Cee; the girl he intended to marry. Why was he forcing her into a position of confrontation?

'I'm sorry,' he said softly, pushing back his chair and coming round the desk towards her. 'I'm a brute; I know. I guess I'm just a bit disappointed. About tomorrow, I mean.' He put his hands on her shoulders, and drew her gently to him. 'Take no notice of me. I'm feeling my age, that's all.'

'Your *age*!' Celia looped her arms around his neck, and gave him a tearful smile. 'You know that's not true. What is it? Is Gallaghers on the brink of bankruptcy or something?'

'It's nothing,' said Reed, his lips against her cheek. 'Put it down to simple bloody-mindedness. Now—do you want me to drive you to the airport? What time is your flight?'

'*The* flight is at eleven-thirty,' Celia replied, emphasising the definite article. 'And if I go, I'll get Daddy to take me. He's flying off to the Common Market conference in the morning. Besides,' she paused, 'I know you hate driving across town in the rush-hour. Remember?'

Reed brushed her lips with his and then let her go. 'I remember,' he conceded evenly. 'When will you be back?'

'Sunday night. But honestly, darling,' Celia gurgled, 'I'd love to have seen your face when Mrs Francis caught you knocking at Antonia's door. I mean—she must have thought the worst!'

Reed's thick lashes lowered. 'That's not what she told you.' It was a statement, not a question.

'No.' Celia conceded the point. 'She just said what you had told her: that you were delivering a message from me.' She shrugged. 'I don't know why you didn't just tell her the truth. It's not as if Antonia is some sort of *femme fatale*. She surely couldn't think you'd be interested in *her*.'

His instincts were to round on her, savagely, for the patronising way she dismissed the other girl, but he held his tongue. 'It was easier to tell her what I did, than explain that I'd forgotten you'd still be at the shop,' he replied lightly. 'Besides, she'd have wondered why I didn't knock at her door first. I don't suppose she regards herself as a nosey old witch!'

'That's because she's not!' protested Celia, laughing all the same. 'And you *should* have knocked at her door first. I mean—you hardly *know* Antonia!'

'I only wanted to use the bathroom, not invite myself in for refreshment!' retorted Reed flatly. 'I didn't think—Antonia would mind. She seemed a pleasant girl.'

'Oh, she is.' Celia adjusted the neckline of her jacket. 'She's sweet. A little *passé* in the way she dresses, perhaps, but that's probably because she doesn't have a lot of money. I mean—she works at some *institute*, where they teach young people—*skills*; that sort of thing. I understand she's not just a shorthand typist, but I doubt if she's paid *awfully* well.'

Reed walked round his desk again. 'Do you like her?'

'*Like* her?' Celia sounded surprised. 'Well—*yes*, I suppose so. I mean, she's not like us, but she's all right. We don't have much in common. I honestly don't know how she *affords* that apartment! It's small, I know, but prices in that area...' Her voice trailed away expressively. Then, as if aware that Reed was waiting for something more, she shrugged. 'Anyway, I don't see much of her. I only asked her to the party because I felt *sorry* for her! And Liz thought I was mad to do it.' She grimaced. 'Actually though, I think that was because Gerry Stockwell seemed so taken with her. Antonia, I mean. Liz was livid!'

Reed pushed his hands into his pockets. 'Stockwell?' he echoed quietly. 'Who is Gerry Stockwell?'

'You know!' Celia fluffed her hair with delicate fingers. 'His father's in steel, or aluminium, something like that. Gerry's the eldest son, *heir* to the family fortune, that sort of thing. Liz says he'll inherit a *title* one day. Anyway, she's been trying to get her claws into him for months, and it was pretty *galling* when he stood and chatted to Antonia for the best part of an hour.'

'As I recall it, she was speaking to several men at once,' Reed remarked levelly. 'No one in particular.'

'No—well, that's true.' Celia outlined her lips with her little finger. 'I mean—you spoke to her yourself, didn't you? Before I realised she was there.'

'No one else was doing so, at that time,' observed Reed drily, flicking back his cuff. Then he drew his features into a polite expression of dismay. 'Heavens, it's nearly five o'clock! Mrs Drysdale will be having fits. I haven't even looked at the letters yet.'

'Oh, aren't you free to go?' Celia looked disappointed. 'I thought you were going to drive me *home*!'

Reed stifled the impulse to refuse point-blank, and made a compromise. 'If you can hang about for another half-hour,' he offered. 'Don't you have to go back to the shop?'

'No. I told Liz I'd go straight home.' Celia sighed. 'Oh, all right. I'll just pop out for a few minutes. There are one or two things I need from the chemist, and that will give you time to sign your letters.'

But after she had gone, Reed did not immediately summon his secretary into the office. Instead, he went to stand by the window—where he seemed to be spending too much time lately, he reflected sourly—and considered the idea, which had entered his head and refused to be dislodged.

The notion of taking Antonia to Stonor with him was a reckless one, he knew. His staff, at his house in Oxfordshire, were trustworthy enough, but he could hardly bring a strange young woman into his home without arousing some comment. It had been different at the apartment. For one thing, Maria had not known who he was asking her to prepare supper for, and even if she had, he acknowledged, she would not have demurred. Maria did not care for Celia. His fiancée's decidedly patronising attitude with people she did not consider her social equal, did not wear well with the German woman, and Maria had already made it clear that she would not be staying on after they were married. Which was a pity, Reed thought, who had known Maria since he was a child at home in Ireland. In those days, she had worked at his family's house in County Wicklow, and he hoped that if she did insist on leaving, his parents might find a place for her again.

He sighed. Maria's future was not in jeopardy for some months yet, and that was not his present problem. What he had to contend with, he acknowledged grimly, was his growing infatuation for a girl who was not his fiancée; a consuming need, that was disturbing his normally easy-going disposition and disrupting his life.

He lifted a hand to massage the muscles of his shoulder with some impatience. He must be crazy, he thought bitterly, recalling all the abortive phone calls he had made to the ground floor flat in Eaton Lodge. During the past week, he had tried to contact Antonia at least a dozen times, and if her phone was not out of order, he could only assume she didn't wish to speak with him.

He shouldn't have warned her, he reflected, re-membering his impulsive promise to ring. If she hadn't known he might be phoning, he would have no reason to suspect that she was avoiding him: and the raw

frustration he felt every time his calls remained
unanswered would have no basis for its inception.

But he had told her, and his inability to get through
was beginning to prey on his nerves. He knew he was
becoming tense, and irritable, and the conversation he
had just had with Celia was an example of his souring
temperament. He had never felt so dissatisfied with his
lot before, and the extent of his self-pity filled him with
contempt. He had to pull himself out of this before he
did something really stupid, he told himself severely,
walking back to his desk. But it was Antonia's image
that filled his mind as he rang for Mrs Drysdale.

Antonia let herself into the flat and leaned back
gratefully against the door. The little carriage clock on
her mantelshelf informed her it was almost eight-thirty,
and she straightened her spine determinedly. She had
approximately fifteen minutes to wash and change her
clothes, and get herself something to eat, if she needed
it. She owed it to Mr Fenwick to turn up for work this
morning, even if it was Friday. He had been kind
enough to give her the time off to go up to Newcastle.
The least she could do was report for work as soon as
she got back.

Of course, her mother had suggested she stay over
until Sunday. 'There's not much point in going back on
a Friday!' she had protested, but Antonia had been
adamant. She felt guilty enough as it was, abandoning
Mr Fenwick for three days at a stretch. And because he
had been so understanding, she didn't want to betray
his trust.

Shaking her head, she pushed herself away from the
door and walked through to her bedroom. She was stiff,
and if she had had more time, she would have
welcomed a bath. Eight hours, cramped in the front of
her cousin Tony's truck, had left her spine feeling as if
she had done it a permanent injury, but she supposed
she should be grateful. He had, at least, saved her her
train fare.

It was not as if her rushing off to Newcastle had

achieved anything, she reflected, stripping off the sweater and jeans she had worn to travel in. But when her mother had rung and said Susie had had an accident, the three hundred miles between them had seemed an interminable distance.

As she washed and cleaned her teeth, Antonia remembered vividly how she had felt when the call had come through on Tuesday morning. Mrs Lord had panicked, and the fact that Susie had fallen off a friend's bicycle and had been taken to hospital with a suspected fractured skull, had sounded reason enough.

As it turned out, Susie spent Tuesday night in the hospital, 'under observation', as the Staff Nurse put it, and returned home on Wednesday, pale, but otherwise unharmed. It was Antonia's mother who had begged her daughter to stay on for at least another night. 'Just in case there are any complications,' she had pleaded, and realising what a shock Mrs Lord had sustained, Antonia had agreed. Susie was *her* daughter, after all. *Her* responsibility, not her mother's.

She managed to get to work on time, and Mr Fenwick looked relieved when he walked into her office and found her already ensconced behind her desk. 'I was half-afraid you wouldn't get back until Monday,' he confessed ruefully. 'And I've got those chaps from the Ministry coming this afternoon.'

'Oh, yes.' Antonia had forgotten the official visit from the education department which had been planned for today. 'Well, I'm here now, so you can relax.'

'Yes.' Mr Fenwick smiled. 'And what about your little girl? How is she?'

'Much better,' said Antonia at once. 'You know what children are like: down one minute, and up the next. They kept her in hospital overnight, but there were no complications, thank goodness. It was my mother who took it hardest. I think she blamed herself.'

'She would,' agreed Mr Fenwick sympathetically. 'Looking after a six-year-old is quite a responsibility for a grandmother. Anyway, I'm glad Susie's all right. I should hate to lose you now.'

'You won't.' Antonia was confident. 'Now—what do you want me to do first? Shall I attend to these estimates, or start on the agenda for next week's meeting?'

Although she had been away and consequently everything in the flat was likely to be stale, Antonia gave up any thought of going shopping at lunchtime. Instead, she collected a sandwich from the dining-hall and ate it at her desk, working right through the break. It was tiring. The disturbed night she had spent in the front of Tony's truck meant she had had little sleep, and it was difficult to keep her eyes open at times. But several cups of strong black coffee served the purpose, and by the time the delegation from the Ministry arrived, she had made some headway with the backlog.

She collected her immediate needs on her way home that afternoon. The buses were full so she walked the distance unhurriedly, enjoying the distinct indications that summer was not as distant as she had thought. The trees were burgeoning with greenness, the birds were twittering in the park; and outside a florist's great bucketfuls of tulips and narcissus nodded their heads as she passed. On impulse, Antonia bought herself a bunch of tulips, inhaling their fresh fragrance as she turned into the gates of Eaton Lodge.

The flowers conjured thoughts of the man, whose image she had been keeping at bay all week, and she permitted herself to wonder if he *had* tried to ring her. The memory of Sunday evening had remained in her subconscious throughout the trauma of the past three days, and while it had not interfered with her anxieties about Susie and her mother, she had not been able to dispel the unworthy suspicion that Reed had played a part in her decision to return so promptly. It was foolish; allowing their association to continue was foolish; but the fact remained, she had thought about him, and to deny it would be less than honest.

The flat looked drab and dusty after its week-long neglect. Tomorrow, she would have to set to and give it a thorough cleaning, she reflected, without enthusiasm, noticing how the sunlight streaming through showed up the murky smudges on the windows. But tonight she was too tired to worry about housework, she decided, pulling out the pre-cooked leg of chicken she had bought for her dinner. After she had eaten, she was going to have an early night. Perhaps tomorrow she would feel more optimistic about tackling her chores.

The sudden knocking at her door interrupted her unpacking of the shopping, and she sighed. Mrs Francis must have seen her come in, she realised wearily. She had had to tell the caretaker she was going away for a few days, and no doubt his wife was curious to hear what had happened.

Suppressing her annoyance, Antonia went to answer the door. It was kind of her to be concerned, she told herself firmly. She ought not to be so ungrateful. But to her astonishment, it was not the garrulous Mrs Francis waiting outside. It was Reed; and her lips parted indignantly when he propelled the door open against her hand and came uninvited into the flat.

'Close it,' he said grimly, when she opened her mouth to make a protest, and she didn't know whether he was referring to her or not. 'The door,' he defined impatiently, and because she really didn't want to attract the caretaker's wife's attention, Antonia complied. But she was furious that he should think he had the right to force his way into her home and it showed.

'Just what do you think you're doing?' she demanded, as he rested against the wall beside the door, and he regarded her with dour intensity.

'That's my question,' he responded, his narrowed eyes moving over her angry face. 'Is your phone out of order?'

'My phone!' Antonia gazed at him blankly. 'I don't know what you mean.'

'Your telephone,' enunciated Reed harshly. 'The instrument people use when they want to get in touch with one another. You do have one, don't you?'

'Of course I do.' Antonia nodded.

'So, why haven't you been answering it?' he enquired oppressively. 'Or does that question require notice?'

Antonia caught her breath. 'You've been *phoning* me!' she exclaimed, suddenly understanding, and he pushed himself away from the wall, a scowl marring his lean features.

'Quick,' he remarked sardonically, his lips twisting. 'I revise my opinion. You're pretty sharp!'

'Oh, don't be so sarcastic!' she retorted, linking and unlinking her fingers. 'I couldn't answer the phone because I haven't been here!'

'No?' He regarded her sceptically. 'Don't tell me they've started a night shift at the institute!'

Antonia flushed at his contemptuous tone. 'No,' she conceded stiffly. 'I haven't been at work.'

Reed expelled his breath heavily. 'So where have you been?'

Antonia held up her head. 'I'm not obliged to tell you.'

'But you will,' he informed her bleakly, moving closer, and her breathing quickened in concert with her accelerating pulse rate.

'Why should I?' she countered, standing her ground. 'It's nothing to do with you.'

'Isn't it?' He was so close now she could see the muscle jerking at the corner of his mouth. 'Not even if I tell you I've been ringing this number constantly since Tuesday evening?'

Antonia moistened her dry lips. 'I didn't ask you to.'

'No.' He conceded the point, his nostrils flaring only slightly as he controlled his temper. 'But the least you could do is be honest with me.'

'I am being honest with you.' Antonia sighed. 'As—as a matter of fact, I went home again.'

'Home?' Reed frowned. 'You mean—to Newcastle?'

'Yes.'

'Oh, come on . . .' He took a backward step. 'You're not trying to tell me you went back to Newcastle on Tuesday, when you only got back from there on Sunday night!'

Antonia blinked. 'Why not?'

He shook his head. 'I wasn't born yesterday, Antonia. If you don't want to tell me where you were, then—I guess I'll have to live with it. But don't *lie* to me!'

'I'm not lying . . .'

'No?'

'No.' She saw his scornful expression and came to a sudden decision. 'My—my daughter had an accident. My mother sent for me.'

Reed's astonishment was palpable. 'Your—*daughter?*'

'Yes.' Antonia straightened her spine. 'I have a child. Now—if you don't mind, I'm very tired . . .'

'Wait a minute.' Reed grasped her arms just below her shoulders. 'You're telling me you've got a daughter? So—where does she live? With your ex-husband?'

'Simon?' Antonia uttered a short laugh. 'No. She lives with my mother. Now, will you please . . .'

'Cool it, will you?' Reed shook her with controlled violence. 'Let me take this in.' He looked down at her impatiently. 'How old is she? What's her name?'

'Susan—*Susie*,' amended Antonia unwillingly. 'And she's six.'

'*Six!*'

'I'm not a teenager, Reed,' she exclaimed, stung by his ejaculation, and his lips turned down ironically.

'I never thought you were,' he assured her drily, and she had to concentrate on the knot of his tie to avoid the disturbing warmth that invaded his eyes. 'I guess I should apologise. For jumping to conclusions, I mean.'

'That's not necessary.'

'Yes, it is.' He sighed. 'What happened? You said she had an accident. Is she all right?'

'She's fine.'

Her tone was as stiff as her spine, and he lifted his shoulders ruefully. 'You don't know what it's been like for me,' he declared. 'I thought you were deliberately ignoring me.'

'A crime, indeed!' she retorted tensely, and his hands slid up over her shoulders to her neck.

'Don't bait me, Antonia,' he advised roughly, his fingers abrasive. 'I mean it. I don't entirely trust my instincts, even if you do look as if you haven't slept for a week!'

Belatedly, Antonia remembered her worn appearance, her pale cheeks and dark-ringed eyes. 'I'm sorry,' she responded bitterly, turning her head aside from his assiduous appraisal. 'This must be quite a shock for you seeing me as I really am! Not to mention discovering I have a child of school age!'

'Antonia——'

His use of her name was a warning, but she paid it no heed. 'What are you doing here anyway?' she demanded wearily, her hands against his stomach providing a necessary barrier. 'Aren't you afraid Celia might see you? Isn't it rather—indiscreet—to come here in daylight?'

'Celia's in Paris,' replied Reed flatly. 'She left this morning and she won't be back until Sunday. Does that answer your question, or would you like more?'

'Oh, no.' Antonia's lips twisted. 'I should have known. You don't take unnecessary risks, do you, Reed?'

'What are you trying to do to me?' he enquired, in a low violent tone. 'What do you want me to say? That I'd come here anyway, and to hell with Cee and our engagement?'

'No——' Antonia coloured.

'Then stop provoking me, will you?' His heated breath fanned her cheek. 'As a matter of fact, I've been sitting out front since about four o'clock, just waiting for you to come home. And that wasn't exactly without hazard!'

Antonia permitted a brief glance up at him. 'You haven't!'

'Oh, I have.' He shrugged. 'Didn't you see the car? It's parked right across the street.' And then he added derisively: 'No. Of course, you wouldn't. I forgot. You were too engrossed in the tulips you were carrying to notice me.'

Antonia shook her head. 'You shouldn't have come here,' she protested, his nearness rapidly overwhelming her objections, as his fingers moved sensuously against her nape. 'You—you should have rung!'

'Again?' he put in wryly, and she had no answer to that.

'Reed . . .'

'Tell me later,' he suggested softly, bending his head to find her resisting lips with his mouth. 'And stop fighting me,' he added, looking down at her splayed palms against his midriff, and with a little moan of helplessness, Antonia slid her arms about his waist.

'We can't do this,' she exclaimed, as his tongue found the delicate cavity of her ear, and he expelled an unsteady breath.

'We're doing it,' he pointed out huskily, his hands sliding into her hair. 'After the week I've had, don't you think I deserve it?'

'I—*no!*' With a supreme effort, Antonia pulled herself away from him, trying to steady her breathing as she ran smoothing hands over her hair. 'Reed—you can't stay here!'

He took a few moments to answer her, but when he did her spirits slumped considerably. 'I don't intend to,' he said, walking round the sofa and subsiding on to the chintz-covered cushions. 'You remember I told you I had a house in the country? I'm going to spend the weekend there.'

'Oh!' Antonia endeavoured not to sound as deflated as she felt. 'I—how nice.'

'It is,' he confirmed, looking up at her with lazily assessing eyes. 'It's just over the Buckinghamshire border into Oxfordshire. Not far from Chalgrove. A village called Stonor's End. My house is just outside the village. Very quiet. Very rural.'

'It sounds lovely.' Antonia forced a note of enthusiasm into her voice.

'Yes.' Reed rested his head back against the upholstery, and sighed. 'It's beautiful at this time of the year. The woods are full of crocuses and there are hundreds of those tulips you admire growing by the lake.'

Antonia moistened her lips. 'There's a lake?'

'Just a small one,' he conceded reflectively. 'We use it for swimming in summer. It's pretty cold, but we enjoy it.'

'We?' Antonia expelled her breath. 'You mean—you and Celia?'

'Occasionally,' he admitted, regarding her through narrowed lids. 'But mostly it's Tricia and her friends who use the place. It's her second home.'

'Tricia?' Antonia frowned. Was she another girl-friend?

'Patricia *Gallagher*,' put in Reed humorously, defining her expression. 'My sister. She's at Oxford. *University*,' he added drily.

'Oh!' Antonia shook her head. 'I see.'

'Do you?' Reed looked sceptical. 'Did you think I kept a harem down there?'

'I never thought about it,' she lied, and he gave her a wry look.

'Anyway, it takes about an hour-and-a-half to get there,' he remarked casually. 'Unless it's the rush hour, and then it can take considerably longer.'

'So why don't you go?' exclaimed Antonia tensely, moving to the hearth to make an unnecessary adjustment to the clock on the mantelshelf. 'It's going to be a fine weekend. At least, that's what Mr Fenwick told me. I'm sure you'll enjoy it.'

'Come with me,' said Reed softly, so softly she thought for a moment she had imagined it. She swung round, her pale face flushed with disbelieving colour, and he pushed himself up from the couch to meet her anxious eyes. 'Come with me,' he said again, pushing his hands into the pockets of his leather jacket. 'Spend the weekend with me. No strings—just a friendly arrangement. I'd like to show you Stonor, and I'd really appreciate your company.'

Antonia blinked. 'You can't be serious!'

Reed sighed. 'Let's not get into another discussion of

what's right and what's wrong,' he said flatly. 'Like I said, I want your company, that's all. I'm not suggesting we share a room or anything crass like that. I like you; and I think that you like me. Why shouldn't we spend some time together?'

CHAPTER SEVEN

ANTONIA's room was at the back of the house, overlooking the terrace and the tennis courts, with the reed-edged sweep of the lake in the background. Immediately below her windows the flagged terrace had a southerly aspect, and beyond a low-walled boundary, manicured lawns sloped down to the water. The wood Reed had spoken of, formed a backdrop in the distance, but nearer at hand there were spreading elms and bushy poplars, breaking up the landscape with their different shades of green.

Antonia leant her elbows on the opened window, hardly noticing the cool morning air through her thin nightgown. It was all so deliciously different from the smell of London, and she inhaled deeply, half-inclined to believe she was still dreaming.

Behind her, the bed she had occupied beckoned invitingly. It was a huge bed, bigger than any she had slept in, even when she was married to Simon. The mattress was modern enough, firm, but delightfully comfortable, and the night before her tired body had appreciated it. But the quilted headboard was decidedly French in appearance, and very much in keeping with the other appointments of the room. The soft-patterned carpet, in muted shades of pink and grey, blended beautifully with the pale grey silk that lined the walls; there were spindley-legged tables beside the bed; a long polished cabinet, inset with drawers, with a mirror above; a *chaise-longue* covered in pale pink velvet with a matching padded stool; and an inlaid rosewood escritoire, ideal for writing letters.

The dusky pink was picked up again in the curtains at the windows and in the thick satin bedspread, that had been turned down for her the night before. Beneath a downy quilt, pale grey silk sheets were

94

quite shamelessly sensual against her skin, and
Antonia remembered how incongruous she had felt
putting on her simple cotton gown. Celia, she was
sure, would wear silk or lace or satin to sleep in. But
then, Celia was used to this kind of treatment; she
was not.

Antonia sighed now, turning away from the window
and surveying the room with some misgivings. Not for
the first time, she wondered what the *real* reaction to
her arrival had been among the other members of the
household. Last night, Reed had introduced her to his
housekeeper, a diminutive woman, by the name of Rose
Macauley, who had been very polite to her. But she
knew that there were other members of staff—Reed's
conversation with his housekeeper had betrayed that—
and Antonia couldn't help acknowledging what she
would think if she was put in their position. What could
they possibly think but the worst? she asked herself
unhappily, wondering if anyone would ever believe that
Reed had not shared her bed.

Not that Reed himself had seemed at all perturbed.
On the contrary, he had got his own way, and in
consequence he was very relaxed and very charming.
His concern for her well-being, his insistence that she
should go to bed as soon as her eyes started drooping,
had made her feel someone very special, and although
she had been a little doubtful, her suspicions had been
ungrounded.

Of course, it had been quite late when they arrived
the night before. It was dark when the Lamborghini
turned between white-painted gates and followed a
gravelled approach to the house. The headlights had
illuminated little beyond the grassy verge that sloped
away at either side, throwing the row of trees into
silhouette, as they formed a shadowy guard along the
drive.

After overcoming her opposition, Reed had suggested
they had dinner in London before driving out to
Stonor's End. That way they would avoid the regular
exodus from the city that generally occurred at

weekends, he explained, and because she had still had
doubts about accompanying him, Antonia had agreed.

But after a delicious meal in a quiet, out-of-the-way
restaurant, with several glasses of wine to augment the
cocktail she had had before she started, Antonia was
too relaxed and too sleepy to offer more than a salutory
protest. Besides, her suitcase was in the boot of the
Lamborghini, alongside Reed's briefcase, and the idea
of spending the weekend in London when she had an
alternative was not appealing. Aware of Reed's
satisfaction when she snuggled down in the seat beside
him, she had felt she ought to be more forceful, but it
hadn't lasted long. Lulled by the warmth of the car, the
lazy music on the radio, and the comforting nearness of
Reed's shoulder, she had felt too contented to resist,
and when she opened her eyes, they were miles along
the motorway.

Their arrival at the house had been achieved with the
minimum amount of fuss. Her own appearance—late in
the evening and probably unannounced—was dealt
with without any particular disturbance, Reed issuing
his orders smoothly, and Mrs Macauley expediting
them with every appearance of co-operation. She had
even smiled and asked about the journey as she showed
Antonia to her room, and if she thought the suitcase
she had insisted on taking charge of was rather big to
transport its lightweight contents, she kept her opinion
to herself.

Antonia supposed she might have felt more embarrassed if she had not been so enthralled by her
surroundings. She had thought Reed's apartment was
impressive, but Stonor House, as it was called, was far
more imposing. Silk carpets; panelled walls; a huge
stained-glass window at the first landing of the fan-
shaped staircase; it was difficult to imagine someone
actually *lived* here. Yet, later, when she had joined Reed
for a drink in the library, she had had to revise her
opinion. Although the walls were lined from floor to
ceiling with leather-bound volumes, and the carpet on
the floor was probably priceless, nevertheless, the room

had a lived-in atmosphere. Apart from the familiar smells of alcohol and good tobacco, the squashy leather chairs that flanked the open fireplace had the comfortably worn appearance of having been well-used, and Reed was there to put her at her ease, with all the teasing eloquence of his race.

Thinking of Reed now, she wondered if he was up yet. It was only eight o'clock and she suspected he would still be in his bed. The idea brought a disturbing awareness to the pit of her stomach, and she went hastily into her bathroom before the disruptive seed could take root.

Like the bedroom the bathroom's decoration was predominantly pink, with smoked glass walls to throw back her reflection from all angles. A round, step-in bath had a jacuzzi fitment, but she decided just to take a shower in case she touched the wrong handles.

Afterwards, she dried her hair with the hand-drier provided, and then wrapping herself in the towelling bathrobe she found behind the door, she returned to the bedroom.

Her clothes were through an archway which opened into a dressing area. There were long mirrors flanking a long, fitted closet where she had hung her few garments the night before. Mrs Macauley had slid one of the long doors aside to show her the vacant space, but now, when she opened the door at the opposite end of the unit, she found herself confronted by a colourful array. They were not her clothes, but they were a woman's clothes, and she closed the door abruptly, and slid back the other panel.

They needn't be Celia's, she told herself severely, as she stepped into tight-fitting jeans and a long-sleeved cotton shirt. *But they could be*, a small voice taunted, and she felt a sudden sickness at the thought that Reed might have shared *her* bed with his fiancée.

She was standing at the mirror which hung above the long cabinet in her bedroom, brushing her hair, when someone knocked at her door. 'Yes?' she called tightly, not sure who it was or what she should do, and the door opened slowly to admit a girl scarcely out of her teens. She was carrying a tray, and she looked in some confusion at the bed when she saw that it was empty. But then she saw Antonia, doing her hair, and her homely features softened to expose a friendly smile.

'Mrs Macauley thought you might prefer breakfast in bed this morning, miss,' she declared, in a lovely Oxfordshire drawl. 'Mr Reed said that you were tired and not to disturb you, but Mrs Macauley thought you might like a cup of tea, it being a strange bed and all.'

'Oh, I would.' Dropping her brush on to the cabinet, Antonia turned to the other girl eagerly. 'How kind of Mrs Macauley.'

'You wouldn't prefer to come downstairs, now you're dressed, would you, miss?' the girl asked doubtfully, but Antonia shook her head. 'Then, I'll put the tray here, shall I?' she suggested, setting it down on the table at the nearside of the bed. 'There's some orange juice, and scrambled eggs too, just in case you're hungry. And Mrs Macauley said if you'd prefer coffee, it's no trouble.'

'The tea is fine,' said Antonia firmly, looking at the beautifully laid-out tray with some bemusement. 'And—and everything else,' she added. 'Thank you. Please tell Mrs Macauley I'm very grateful.'

'Yes, miss.'

The girl smiled and departed, and Antonia approached the tray with some amazement. The orange juice was freshly squeezed, and resided in a cut-glass container; the scrambled eggs nestled beneath a silver cover; curls of butter and lightly browned toast jostled a dish of strawberry preserve; and the bone-china teacup and saucer stood beside a squat bone-china teapot, fitted with a padded velour cosy.

Antonia shook her head and sat down on the side of the bed to pour herself some tea. It was years since anyone had brought her breakfast in bed, and never had it been set out so attractively; and although she rarely swallowed more than a slice of toast before leaving for work in the morning, she couldn't resist sampling the orange juice and the eggs.

As she had anticipated, the juice was sweet and palatable, and took no effort whatsoever. The eggs, too, were light and fluffy, and despite her intention just to taste them, she found herself eating with enthusiasm. It must be the air, she told herself wryly, spreading strawberry preserve on a slice of toast. She couldn't ever remember enjoying a breakfast so much.

By the time she had finished the meal, and applied a little make-up, it was after nine o'clock, a much more respectable hour, she reflected. Checking her appearance before leaving the room, she was relieved to see the dark lines that had surrounded her eyes the day before had almost disappeared, and there was actually a little colour in the skin that covered her cheekbones. Her newly washed hair gleamed with health, and although she found her features ordinary, anticipation leant an unfamiliar sparkle to her eyes.

Leaving the tray, and her unmade bed—an unheard-of luxury—Antonia opened her door and looked along the wide corridor. She knew the staircase was to her right. The night before, when Mrs Macauley had shown her to her room, she had taken especial notice of the fact that they had turned left at the top of the stairs so that later, when she wanted to go to bed, she did not need Reed's escort to take her there.

Now, closing the door behind her, she trod the soft cream carpet to the head of the stairs. Several other doors opened off the corridor, and she wondered if one of them was Reed's. If her room was the one Celia used, it was quite likely, she thought, remembering the dismay she had felt earlier, before the maid had brought her breakfast. But as there was a matching corridor at the opposite side of the staircase, it was debatable. Would Reed be so unsubtle as to situate his and his fiancée's rooms side by side, she mused unwillingly, when he must know what interpretation would be put upon it?

The glossy wood of the banister rail ran silkily beneath her fingers as she descended the stairs. Below her, the shining expanse of polished wood revealed a

conscientious attention to duty, the steady tick of a
grandfather clock the only sound to disturb the silence.
Unless one listened hard, she acknowledged; then one
could hear the birds, and the distant barking of a dog,
and even the lowing of cattle, grazing somewhere not
too far away.

'Are you looking for someone, Miss Sheldon?'
inquired a businesslike voice behind her, and Antonia
realised she had been standing on the bottom stair, like
someone in a dream.

'Oh—Mrs Macauley,' she exclaimed, finding the tiny
housekeeper at her elbow. 'I—is Mr Gallagher up yet? I
was just wondering where I might find him.'

'Sure, Mr Reed was up two hours ago, Miss
Sheldon,' responded Mrs Macauley, revealing a brogue
Antonia had scarcely identified the night before. 'He
said you'd be sleeping till mid-morning most likely, but
I thought you might find it strange here, after the
clamour of London.'

'And you were right.' Antonia smiled. 'I should
thank you again for my breakfast. It was delicious. I . . .
er . . . I left the tray upstairs.'

'That's all right, Miss Sheldon. Ruth will get it when
she goes to make the bed.'

'Um—it's *Mrs* Sheldon, actually,' murmured
Antonia, a little awkwardly. 'Do—do you know
where—Reed is?'

Mrs Macauley did not immediately respond to her
enquiry. '*Mrs* Sheldon, is it?' she remarked noncommit-
tally. 'And will your husband be joining us, Mrs
Sheldon?'

'No.' Antonia was obliged to answer her. 'I'm
divorced, Mrs Macauley, and I don't know where my
ex-husband is.'

'Ah . . .' The housekeeper cupped her elbow in the
palm of one hand and tugged thoughtfully at her ear
with the other. 'You're young to be looking for another
husband, Mrs Sheldon.'

'I'm not looking for another husband, Mrs
Macauley,' retorted Antonia shortly, rapidly revising

her opinion of Reed's choice of retainer. 'Do you know Mr Gallagher's whereabouts, or shall I look for him myself?'

'Sure, he's been out with the horses since half-past seven,' responded the housekeeper at once. 'And if you're planning on going down to the stables, I should put a coat on, if I were you. The sun's out, but there's still a nip in the air.'

'Thank you.'

Antonia's acknowledgment was decidedly frosty, and the housekeeper smiled. 'Sure, I'm only thinking of the good of—*both* of you,' she observed sagely. 'Wrap up warm now. You wouldn't be wanting to get a chill, now, would you?'

Collecting her pale blue anorak from her room, Antonia had to admit it was difficult to remain aggrieved with Mrs Macauley. The woman said outrageous things, it was true, but Antonia sensed she really did have Reed's well-being at heart. No doubt it was the housekeeper's way of warning her off, Antonia reflected uneasily. And after all, she must be curious as to why her employer had brought a strange young woman into his home. It would be different if there were several guests; but there weren't. There was only her, and the fact that she was divorced led to obvious speculation.

Downstairs again, in the absence of any known alternative, Antonia let herself out of the front door, and pushing her hands into the pockets of her jacket, set off across the courtyard. Mrs Macauley had been right, she thought, as a chill breeze swept her hair back from her face. It was much cooler than it had been the night before, and although the sun was shining, it was not making any impact.

The front of the house faced down the drive they had driven up the night before, and now Antonia could see the imposing sweep of grassland that stretched as far as the distant gateposts. To her right, white rails fenced in a handful of mares and their foals, and further afield, the cattle she had heard earlier grazed a lush green pasture. Like Reed had said, it was very peaceful and very rural, and she filled her lungs with enthusiasm as she breathed the country air.

At one end of the long row of windows that confronted her, a wall, inset with an arched doorway, gave access to the garage yard. The Lamborghini was there, being hosed down by a boy of about sixteen, but he turned off the water at Antonia's approach, and arched his brows rather insolently. 'Did you want something?'

'Yes. Mr Gallagher,' replied Antonia, with some reluctance. 'I'm looking for the stables actually. Is this the way?'

'You'd be—Miss Sheldon, is that right?' enquired the boy inquisitively, squeezing out his wash-leather in a bucket standing close by, and Antonia sighed.

'Mrs Sheldon, yes,' she agreed, glancing impatiently about her. 'Can I get to the stables this way?'

The boy hesitated, obviously wishing he could say more, but unlike Mrs Macauley, he did not have the confidence. 'Yes,' he said off-handedly, nodding towards another gateway across the yard. 'If you go through there and follow the path, you'll see the stables right ahead of you.'

'Thank you.'

Antonia followed his instructions, aware as she did so that his eyes followed her until she was out of the gate. No doubt he was wondering exactly what her relationship with Reed was, she reflected, wishing she had anticipated this before she agreed to come.

But then, she thought, she had not realised just how many people were going to be involved. Her visions of Reed's country house might have run to a domestic of some kind, like at his apartment in London. She had not forseen a country manor, with all its incumbent employees.

She saw Reed before she reached the three-sided collection of buildings that made up the stable block. He was in the yard, talking with an elderly man, who Antonia assumed must be the groom, and her heart accelerated annoyingly at the sight of his lean frame. In a suede jerkin and matching moleskin trousers, pushed into knee-length black boots, he looked perfectly at ease with his surroundings. The cream knitted sweater he was wearing, whose rolled collar brushed his chin, accentuated the darkness of his complexion, but otherwise he looked like an English country squire, returning from an outing with the hunt.

The old man saw Antonia first, and apparently he drew Reed's attention to it, for he turned and gave her a casual wave. What did he think he was doing? Antonia asked herself unhappily, slowing her step. How was he going to explain this visit—no matter how innocent—to Celia? And how was she likely to react to the fact that her downstairs neighbour was attracting far too much attention from the man she herself intended to marry? Reed could not expect to keep this a secret. Not when people like Mrs Macauley and the boy who had been cleaning the Lamborghini were so evidently intrigued by her identity. If she were Celia, she would resent it; was she any better than Simon, after all?

Halting at the edge of the cobbled stable yard, she stamped her feet in their dark blue trainers. She shouldn't have come. That was all there was to it. She could fool herself that she wasn't harming anyone, but she really shouldn't have come.

'What are you looking so fed-up about?' enquired Reed tolerantly, detaching himself from the groom, and strolling lazily towards her. 'I didn't think you'd be up yet. Didn't you sleep well?'

'I slept very well,' replied Antonia formally, her shoulder lifting to dislodge the hand he had laid upon it. And, because it was expected of her, she added: 'Did you?'

'No. As a matter-of-fact, I slept badly,' Reed responded softly. 'For which you can take the credit.' His lips twisted. 'Have you had breakfast?'

'Yes.' Antonia made a dismissive gesture. 'Mrs Macauley sent me breakfast in bed. Unfortunately, I was already up when it arrived.'

'I told her not . . .'

'Yes, so the maid said,' Antonia interrupted him tensely. 'But I'm not used to lying in bed until all hours. I'm a working woman.'

'So you keep reminding me,' remarked Reed drily. 'Now—would you like to look round? I don't know if you're interested in horses, but I keep a couple of hunters.'

'A *couple*!' Antonia glanced back over her shoulder. 'I saw at least twice that number in the paddock.'

'They're breeding mares,' responded Reed carelessly. 'Charlie Lomax, he's my trainer, he likes to keep a few mares in foal, just to keep his hand in. He used to run a stud farm, before he came to work for me. I'll show you the foals, if you like. They're very friendly.'

'No. That is——' Antonia looked down at her feet as she struggled to find the words. 'Reed, I'd better go back.'

His grey eyes narrowed. 'Back where? To the house?' He frowned. 'Is something wrong?'

'I mean—back to London,' she admitted unhappily, and he smothered a savage oath.

'For Christ's sake,' he swore, in a low voice, 'I thought we'd settled that!'

'Well, we haven't,' she mumbled, pushing her hair back out of her eyes. 'Reed, I feel such a fraud! I don't belong here.'

'Who says so?' he enquired, his features hardening. 'Did Rose say something? Did anyone else make any insinuations?'

'Well, no—at least, not exactly.'

'What's that supposed to mean?'

Antonia scuffed her toe against the cobbles. 'Mrs Macauley kept calling me *Miss* Sheldon, so I told her I was divorced.'

'And?' His eyes were intent.

'Oh——' Antonia sighed. 'Does it matter?'

'It does to me.' He paused. 'Are you telling me Rose made some comment about you being a divorcee?'

'Well, she said . . . she said I was young to be looking

for another husband,' admitted Antonia at last. 'I don't think she believed me when I said I wasn't.'

'Is that all?' Reed's expression softened again. 'Oh, take no notice of Rose. She's curious, that's all.'

'Wouldn't you be?' exclaimed Antonia, not responding to his mocking smile. 'Reed, can you imagine what these people must be thinking? I'm half-inclined to believe she sent my breakfast to bed to see if we were sharing the same room!'

'What? With me out with the horses soon after seven?' asked Reed teasingly, and her colour deepened. 'Antonia, if we were sleeping together, we'd still be in bed. Believe me, I would not be venting my frustration on a dumb animal!'

Antonia's breath caught in her throat. 'You shouldn't say things like that.'

'Why not? They're true.' His hands descended on her shoulders, and uncaring of the old man still pottering about in the yard behind him, he jerked her towards him. 'Just because I've agreed to your terms, doesn't mean I have to approve of them,' he told her huskily, his mouth warmly insistent on hers. 'Now, come on: stop all this nonsense about rushing back to London, and let me show you the grounds. *I* want you here. That's what's important.' He let her go with some reluctance, and captured her hand in his. 'I'll even let you pick some crocuses in the wood, if you promise to be good.'

Antonia shook her head, but she was weakening, and he knew it. 'Reed—what about Celia? What will she say when——?'

'Let me worry about Celia,' he informed her flatly. Then, observing her uncertainty, he shook his head. 'Stop anticipating something that may never happen.' He smiled. 'Now—do you want to take the dogs? I warn you, they're very affectionate—just like their master.'

It was a wonderful morning. Accompanied by two excitable retrievers, who spent most of their time gambolling in the grass, Antonia walked for miles.

Wearing a pair of rubber boots Reed found for her in the stables, she kept pace with him across the paddock—where the foals dogged their progress—and into the pasture, with its doe-eyed collection of cattle. It didn't matter where she put her feet in the rubber boots, which was just as well in the circumstances, and Reed doubled up when she fastidiously cleaned her boots after every unwary step.

'So long as you don't make a mistake and sit down in it,' he teased her, his hand running possessively over her rear, and she met his gaze in sudden confusion, before brushing his hand away.

They talked a lot; impersonal things mostly, although Reed did tell her a little about the company, and the role he played in it. He was offhand about his own qualifications, playing down the first he had got at Oxford, the agile brain, which had absorbed so much information about the company's operations while he was still in his teens. Yet, Antonia sensed the pride he had in his family's traditions, his admiration for the prestige which his father and his grandfather had maintained, their success in a world where it wasn't always easy just to survive.

She was fascinated by his grasp of investment and finance, but although she listened avidly when he spoke of the company's accomplishments overseas, she was once again reminded of their very different backgrounds. Reed had grown up, secure in the knowledge that one day Gallaghers would be in his control; a multi-million dollar company, with all its incumbent responsibilities. She, on the other hand, was the daughter of a mining overseer from Tyneside, who had been killed in an accident at the pit, when Susie was only a baby.

They had lunch in the breakfast room, an attractive room, overlooking the terrace. After their walk, Antonia's cheeks were flushed with becoming colour, and Reed seldom took his eyes from her as she ate her meal with real enjoyment.

'It's just as well I'm only staying until tomorrow,' she

exclaimed, swallowing a mouthful of the succulent steak and kidney pie that Reed had explained his cook, Mrs Braid, had prepared for them. She smiled delightfully. 'I'd get awfully fat! Just like Tuppence.'

'Who is Tuppence?' enquired Reed lazily, neglecting his own meal and resting his elbows on the table.

'He's a cat,' admitted Antonia ruefully. 'My mother's cat, actually. Susie torments him unmercifully.'

Reed cupped his chin on one hand. 'I'd like to meet Susie,' he said, disconcerting her still further. 'Can I?'

Antonia put down her knife and fork. 'How can you?' she countered, looking down at her plate. 'I've told you. She lives with my mother.'

'In Newcastle. I know.' Reed stretched across the table to take one of her hands in his. 'But you go home sometimes, don't you? At weekends,' he prompted drily.

Antonia tried to draw her fingers away, but he wouldn't let her, and looking up at him, she said: 'Why do you want to meet her?'

'Because she's yours,' replied Reed evenly. 'Because I'd like to know her, when you talk about her. Because she's part of your life.'

Antonia sighed. 'Oh, Reed——'

'Oh, Reed—nothing,' he told her softly. 'How about next weekend? I could drive you up there on Friday night—or Saturday morning, if you'd prefer it. Don't worry,' he added, as her eyes grew anxious, 'I'm not inviting myself to your mother's house. I can stay at an hotel.' He grinned. 'I presume there are hotels in Newcastle, aren't there?'

'Of course, there are.' Antonia was indignant, until she saw his teasing smile. 'But—well, I don't know if my mother would like that. Your staying in an hotel, I mean. She'd think—well, you can guess what she'd think, I'm sure.'

'That her home wasn't good enough?' enquired Reed, with a grimace. 'Sweetheart, if you invited me to stay with you, I'd be only too happy to accept.'

'Don't be silly!' Antonia was confused, as much by

his casual use of the endearment as by his outrageous suggestion. What he was proposing was wild; *reckless*; almost as reckless as her being here at Stonor's End.

'Wouldn't you like to go home next weekend?' he asked, playing with her fingers, and she drew an uneven breath.

'What would I tell my mother?'

'Do you have to tell her anything?'

Antonia shook her head. 'How do I introduce you?'

Reed shrugged. 'As a—friend. What's so unusual about that?'

Antonia bent her head. 'A *rich* friend!'

'A *friend*,' he amended harshly. 'Antonia, stop putting the obstacle of my being a Gallagher between us!' He lifted her hand to his lips and she felt his tongue against her palm. 'Let me come with you,' he said huskily. 'Let me meet Susie. I promise I won't do anything to embarrass you.'

Mrs Macauley's arrival with their dessert saved Antonia from making a response. But Reed's eyes were frankly persuasive as they dwelt upon her face, and Antonia snatched her hand away in embarrassment before meeting the housekeeper's knowing gaze.

'Mrs Sheldon approves of your choice of menu, Rose,' Reed remarked incorrigibly, as the housekeeper cleared their plates. 'That's right, isn't it, Antonia? You did enjoy Mrs Braid's pride and joy!'

'I—the pie was lovely,' Antonia conceded uncomfortably. 'I don't think I could eat another thing.'

'I'm sure you'll find room for a few fresh raspberries,' responded Mrs Macauley drily, her sharp eyes missing nothing in their exchange. She set a dish of raspberries and a jug of cream on the table. 'Will you have coffee here, or in the drawing room?'

'We'll have it in the sitting room,' replied Reed, pushing the fruit towards Antonia. 'Help yourself,' he added. 'I like watching you.'

Antonia flushed then; she couldn't help it; and Mrs Macauley regarded her half-sympathetically. 'Take no notice of him, Mrs Sheldon,' she remarked, with the

familiarity of long service. 'If you want some—have
some. He hasn't eaten a decent meal since he came
here.'

She departed on this note, and Antonia looked
doubtfully across the table. 'Is that true?'

Reed grimaced. 'We've only been here since last
night!'

'Didn't you have any breakfast either?'

'I'm not hungry,' he responded quietly. 'At least—not
for food,' he added disturbingly. Then, as if realising he
was getting too serious, he forced a smile. 'Have some
raspberries. Just to please me.'

They spent the afternoon in the sitting room,
listening to music and watching the changing weather
outside. Contrary to Mr Fenwick's expectations, it had
begun to rain while they were having lunch, and now
the drops pattering at the windowpanes enclosed them
in a world cut off from outside influences.

Antonia had found that Reed's taste in music was
similar to her own, a mixture of contemporary bands
and traditional jazz. They both liked China Crisis and
Duran Duran, but they also enjoyed Count Basie and
Duke Ellington, and Antonia discovered other favour-
ites like Elton John and Lionel Richie among the
enormous collection of albums stacked beneath the hi-fi
system.

Curled up on the floor in her jeans and sweater and
without any make-up, she was totally unaware of how
young she appeared. It was only when she looked up
and found Reed's gaze upon her that she realised she
had forgotten to be on her guard with him, and she
brushed her hair out of her eyes in a purely defensive
gesture.

'Relax,' he said, seeing the sudden consternation that
crossed her face at this awareness. 'You're enjoying
yourself, aren't you?'

'You know I am,' she admitted, unknowingly
sensuous as she stretched her arms above her head, and
Reed shifted on the soft rug.

'I'm sleepy,' he said, lowering his length at right

angles to her and depositing his head in her lap. 'Do you mind?' he murmured, but it was a rhetorical question. His eyes were already closed, and she hadn't the will to refuse him.

He did sleep for a while, she thought, his head growing heavier on her legs. With his eyes closed, his face had a disturbing vulnerability, and she couldn't resist the urge to smooth the silky dark hair back from his forehead. He didn't move, the splayed fan of his lashes a dusky arc above his cheekbones. It made her reckless; it made her want to touch him in other places; and her fingers slid daringly over his ear to the heavy roll collar of his sweater.

He stirred then, his eyes opening to look up into hers. Then, lifting his arms, he took her hand and pushed it inside the neck of his sweater, letting her fingers feel his warmth and the lean hard strength beneath his skin. It was an unnerving experience, an unfamiliar intimacy that brought with it a quickening of her pulses and a wash of hot colour to her cheeks. His skin felt so supple, so masculine, the scent of his body unmistakably aroused. For a moment, she held his gaze, feeling her own response like a physical ache in the pit of her stomach. Then, abruptly, she pulled her hand away and scrambled to her feet.

His head thudded on to the rug at her hasty withdrawal, but she didn't apologise. Instead, she went to sit on the seat by the window, and by the time she had controlled herself sufficiently to glance behind her, Reed had resumed his position with his back against the patterned sofa.

The maid who had brought Antonia's breakfast that morning, appeared with afternoon tea at about five o'clock. Antonia, who had spent the last half-hour gazing out at the windswept paddock, abandoned her seat by the window to return to an armchair at the girl's appearance, and Reed smiled at the maid as she set the tray beside her.

'Hello, Ruth,' he said, his tone revealing nothing but a friendly interest. 'How is your mother? Is she any better?'

'Oh, yes, Mr Reed.' Ruth straightened from her task and gazed at him with evident pleasure. 'That holiday really bucked her up. Doctor Michaels says there's no reason why she shouldn't make a full recovery.'

'That's good.' Reed nodded, and Antonia averted her eyes from his attractive face. 'Tell her I was asking after her, will you? Oh, and get George to give you some of those hyacinths out of the greenhouse.'

'Thank you.' Ruth coloured with pride. 'I'll do that.'

'Good.'

Reed regarded her good-humouredly, and with a little nod at Antonia, the girl made a hasty retreat.

Alone again, Antonia forced herself to look at him. 'You like your tea without milk, don't you?' she asked, noticing the slices of lemon residing on a dish.

'Please,' he conceded, putting aside the record sleeve he had been reading. 'You remembered? That's something, I suppose.'

'Reed, please——'

'I know, I know,' he said shortly, evidently finding it less easy to be civil with her. His grey eyes narrowed sardonically. 'I'm sorry. It won't happen again.'

And it didn't. For the remainder of the time they were at Stonor, Reed was on his best behaviour, sustaining a friendly—if impersonal—relationship, that Antonia told herself she wanted, but which was very hard to take after their earlier closeness.

But what did she want, after all, if not to maintain a certain distance between them? she asked herself impatiently, when on Saturday evening Reed abandoned her after dinner, on the pretext of checking on one of his mares that was in foal. How could she expect to go with him, out into the darkness of the stableyard and subsequently, into the warm shadowy intimacy of the stables themselves? she argued fiercely. There would be too many awkward moments, too many opportunities to surrender to the guilty feelings that lay so shallowly beneath the veneer of her detachment. But when, at ten

CHAPTER EIGHT

REED drove her back to London on Sunday evening.

It was still light when they left Stonor's End, and Antonia looked back over her shoulder with a helpless sense of despair. It hardly seemed possible it was only two days since he had brought her here. Already she felt an affinity with the house that was going to be difficult to displace.

The day itself had been something of an anti-climax, in that Reed had not appeared before lunchtime. Mrs Macauley, taking pity on her, as she mooched about the downstairs rooms that morning, had declared Reed had been up half the night with the vet, attending to the mare, whose foal had been born feet first. But Antonia had guessed that the housekeeper, too, had her doubts, and one sort of speculation was just as bad as another.

In the afternoon, Reed had spent more precious time talking with George Hetherington, the gardener. Antonia had seen them from her bedroom window, when she had gone upstairs to pack, and she had stood for several minutes watching them, feeling as if her heart was being torn out of her. She didn't want to go; it was as simple as that. She didn't want to return to London, knowing that when she left him, she might never see him again.

The maid, Ruth, had been changing Antonia's bed when she first entered the bedroom, and she had offered to pack for her. 'It's all right; I can manage,' Antonia told her gratefully. 'You go on with what you're doing. I shan't get in your way.'

Ruth smiled her thanks. 'You're leaving today, are you, miss?' she asked, rapidly changing pillow slips. 'Do you like living in London?'

'Not a lot.' Antonia was honest. 'But some of us don't have a choice.'

'No.' Ruth set the pillows squarely against the padded headboard. 'I sometimes think I'd like to live in London, but what with Mum and all, I don't think that's likely.'

'Your mother's been ill?' asked Antonia sympathetically. 'I'm sorry. Was it something serious?'

'Cancer,' said Ruth grimacing. 'She had to have an operation. Then lots of therapy—you know, to make sure all the cells were dead. She was pretty sick over Christmas. My dad didn't think she'd make it.'

'But she did.' Antonia regarded the girl gently.

'Oh, yes.' Ruth's smile reappeared. 'Thanks to Mr Reed. He arranged everything—all the treatment, the nursing home, everything! Then, when she was fit enough, he sent her and my dad out to Barbados for a holiday. Just so's she'd get away from the cold weather.'

Antonia took a deep breath. 'That was kind of him.'

'Well, he is, isn't he?' said Ruth artlessly. 'But I expect you know that. Being a friend of his, and all.'

Antonia had made some comment, she didn't remember what, and soon afterwards, Ruth had finished her task and left her. But her words stuck in Antonia's mind, not least because of their honesty. Reed *was* kind, and generous, and she had never known a man like him before.

The journey back to London was accomplished without any delays, and it was barely a quarter to nine when the Lamborghini drew to a halt outside the gates of Eaton Lodge. Reed had not suggested stopping for dinner on their way, indeed, he had scarcely spoken at all during the journey, and Antonia assumed he would be glad to see the back of her.

However, he surprised her by insisting on carrying her suitcase to her door, dismissing her fears about Mrs Francis with the careless information that she generally went to her daughter's on Sundays.

Struggling to get her key into the lock, Antonia wondered why he simply hadn't dumped her and her suitcase at the gate. He was obviously keen to leave her, so she didn't offer him a drink. With the door open behind her, she opened her mouth to express her thanks for his hospitality, when he suddenly said flatly: 'I suppose you're not going to invite me to Newcastle next weekend, are you?'

'I——' Antonia could hardly speak. 'I—do you—still want to come?'

'I still want—everything,' he told her harshly, and as the foolish tears welled into her eyes, he backed her into the flat and slammed the door behind them.

His arms were around her before the latch had clicked into place, and his mouth found hers with hungry urgency. Almost without her volition, it seemed, her arms were around his neck, her fingers sliding into the hair at his nape, her lips parting under his tongue. She wanted him; she admitted it to herself; and as he went on kissing her, all her previous objections melted, like her bones.

'Oh, God,' he muttered at last, and she realised, with a pang, that he was trembling, too. 'What are you trying to do to me?'

'I—I thought you wanted to go. I thought you were sick of me,' she stammered unsteadily, her lips against his neck, and he groaned.

'You said—hands off, remember?' he reminded her roughly, his face grim as he looked down at her. 'If you'd changed your mind, you should have let me know sooner.'

Antonia gasped. 'That's a rotten way to put it!'

'What do you expect?' he demanded violently. 'I'm not used to spending two whole days in a permanent state of frustration!'

'Oh, no, of course not.' Antonia gazed up at him bitterly, anger taking the place of submission. 'I forgot. You're used to an entirely different reaction!'

'Yes, I am,' he told her brutally, and pulling her unresisting arms from around his neck, he stepped back from her. 'I'd better go. I've got some work to do before I go to bed.'

Antonia turned away, unwilling for him to see the

anguish his words had evoked, and she heard the distinctive click as the door closed behind him. '*Damn, oh, damn,*' she breathed, feeling a wave of misery sweeping over her, and after assuring herself that she really was alone, she ran into her bedroom and flung herself on the bed. The things she ought to be doing, like unpacking her clothes, or catching up with the housework she had not done since before she went to Newcastle, were forgotten. Instead, she gave in to the aching need to express the pain inside her.

The depression of the mattress was the first indication she had that she was no longer alone, and a blind panic gripped her as hands touched her body. Catching back a cry, she jerked away, rolling over on to her back in an effort to identify her intruder.

But the cry died in her throat when she saw the man sitting on the bed beside her. 'Y-you!' she got out chokily. 'What—what are you doing here?' She scrubbed her knuckles across eyes which she was sure were red and puffy. 'How did you get in?'

Her key dangled confusingly from his hand, and he dropped the offending article on to the bureau beside her bed. 'You left it in the lock outside,' Reed told her wryly, evading her efforts to keep his hands at bay, and smoothing the damp tendrils of hair out of her eyes. 'It was just as well you did. I'm not much good at breaking down doors.'

Antonia moved her head from side to side. 'You— you left——'

'I got as far as the car,' he contradicted her huskily, his thumbs disposing of two errant streaks of dampness on her cheeks. 'Stop fighting me, will you? I may have saved you from an unwelcome intruder.'

'Who—who says you're welcome?' Antonia demanded, turning her head away, and with a muffled oath, he shrugged off his jacket and stretched his length beside her on the bed.

'I do,' he affirmed, capturing her face with one hand and bringing her mouth to his. 'What do you want me to say?' he added, covering her face with hot urgent

kisses. 'That I'm sorry? You know I am. That I've kept
out of your way since Saturday because I couldn't bear
to be near you and not touch you? You know it's the
truth!'

Antonia shook her head. 'I know you shouldn't be
here——'

He paused then, drawing back to look at her, the
lines of strain sharply etched beside his mouth. 'Do
you want me to go?' he asked tensely, pushing his
fingers into her hair, his hands moving sensuously
against her scalp, and she knew she couldn't send him
away again.

'I—*no*,' she admitted honestly, lifting her hand to his
lean face and allowing him to turn her palm against his
lips. 'Oh, no,' she said again, slipping her arms around
his neck, and with a shuddering sigh, he found her
mouth once more . . .

Afterwards, it was difficult to remember anything but
the intense pleasure he had given her. She knew he had
undressed her. She could recall the possessive intimacy
of his hands as they had caressed her limbs through the
frustrating barrier of her clothes, her breasts swelling
and hardening beneath the insinuating brush of his
exploring thumbs. She had wanted to tear her clothes
from her then, and his from him, but in the event, Reed
had disposed of that obstacle with infinite patience.

He had removed his own clothes with rather less
deliberation, Antonia's instinctive lips and fingers
driving him to abandon his control. In only a few
seconds he was beside her again, his lean supple limbs
entwining with hers as his mouth sought the provocative
arousal of a dusky pink nipple.

His body was every bit as brown and muscled as she
had anticipated, and she revelled in the delights of being
able to do with him as she willed. The hungry urgency
of their passion was tempered by the pleasure they took
in one another, and Reed's tongue ravished her mouth
in imitation of the possession he was to exact later.

'You're beautiful,' he told her huskily, imprisoning

her arms above her head, and straddling her body so that he could look down at her.

'So are you,' she breathed, her hands straying tantalisingly down over his flat stomach, and with a groan he subsided upon her.

'I want you,' he said unsteadily, his breath moistening her ear, and she quivered.

'I want you,' she confessed, her arms closing convulsively about him, and his mouth crushed hers with hungry passion.

It was strange, she thought now, in the aftermath, how instinctively he had known how to please her. By the time the pulsating strength of his body had penetrated hers, she was aching for his possession, and all the occasions Simon had clumsily taken his pleasure were erased by the simple act of Reed's possession. There was no pain with Reed, no hasty satiation of his senses, no selfish betrayal of her needs as a woman. Instead, he had *made love* to her, something she now realised Simon had never done, and in so doing he had taken them both to the outer limits of human experience.

She knew he had felt the uncontrollable release of feeling, too. The shuddering spasms that racked his body when he attained that final peak with her were proof enough, without the sensual warmth of him inside her. For the first time in her life, she acknowledged the fact that she was not cold or frigid as Simon had accused her of being. She was, instead, a sensitive, passionate woman, who had only just recognised her own sensuality.

It was dark in the room now, and she shivered as the coolness of the air around them chilled her flesh. Wriggling out from beneath the weight of Reed's supine body, she grasped a handful of the quilt and pulled it around her, wondering with an unwilling sense of apprehension exactly what time it was.

'Don't go,' objected Reed sleepily, capturing her hand and drawing it to his lips, but the air was cooling more than just Antonia's skin.

'It's late. *You* have to go,' she told him unevenly, and detaching herself from him, she abruptly switched on the bedside lamp.

If she expected the sudden illumination to embarrass him, she was wrong. Making no effort to cover himself, he rolled lazily on to his back, and lay regarding her unnervingly through the fringe of his lashes.

'Do you want me to?' he enquired at last, propping himself up on one elbow, and Antonia swallowed convulsively.

'It—it's not what I want, is it?' she got out jerkily, hating the need to remind him of that fact, and hating the connotations her words had evoked. 'Your—your car's outside. Anyone can see it.'

'So?' His eyes dwelt sensually on her mouth. 'I told you. I have a key for Cee's flat.'

Antonia shook her head. 'But—you said she's coming back tonight.'

'Let me worry about that,' he advised her huskily, stroking long fingers down the length of her calf, but Antonia stumbled off the bed, dragging the quilt with her.

'You—you're completely unscrupulous, aren't you?' she choked, rounding on him. 'What possible excuse can you produce for your car standing out there all evening? Don't you care what Celia will think of you? Don't you care what she'll think of me?'

'Not right now,' he informed her steadily, and as she struggled to tear her eyes away from his powerful body, he came up off the bed and tugged the protective quilt from her. 'Oh, love,' he breathed, his hands on her hips making her irresistibly aware that he was anything but satisfied at this moment. 'Let me stay. Let me sleep with you. I don't want to go home. I want to make love to you—all night, if that were possible. And you're the *only* woman I've ever said that to.'

Naturally, Antonia overslept. By the time her exhausted eyes opened to take a dazed assessment of the time, it was already after nine o'clock, and the sun was streaming busily through the cracks in the curtains.

Gasping, she struggled up on her pillows, but the imprisoning weight of Reed's arm and the leg that lay confidingly between hers made it an effort.

'Relax,' he grumbled protestingly, opening his eyes to find her face already flushed with her exertions. 'It's early yet.'

'It's a quarter-past-nine,' she contradicted him huskily, her breathing constricting as he bestowed a lingering kiss at the corner of her mouth. 'Reed—I was due at work at nine o'clock. I've got to go!'

He sighed. 'Take the day off.'

'No.' It was a temptation, but she resisted it. 'I—Mr Fenwick was kind enough to give me the time off last week when Susie was ill. I can't let him down again.'

Reed grimaced. 'Okay, okay.' He responded to her panic-stricken efforts to be free by releasing her. 'But——' his hand brushed gently across her cheek, 'I hope he's not as perceptive as I am.'

Antonia paused in the process of sliding out from under the quilt. 'What do you mean?' she asked, and Reed's lips parted in a teasing grin.

'The way you look,' he informed her lazily, and she frowned.

'The way I look?' she echoed. 'Do I look that bad?'

Reed laughed. 'You don't look—bad—at all. At least, not in the sense you mean.'

'Reed!'

'All right.' He sobered. 'You look—ravishing; or should I say ravished?' His lips tilted. 'My darling, you look as if you've spent the night doing what we have been doing. And it suits you.'

Antonia's cheeks were scarlet when she permitted herself a brief glance at her reflection in the dressing table mirror. All she could see were the dark rings around her eyes, evidence of the disturbed night she had spent, and she saw nothing appealing in the vulnerable curve of her mouth.

'I don't want to leave you,' murmured Reed softly, coming up behind her and drawing her resisting body back against his. His hands slid round her body to

cover her breasts, and their peaks hardened automatically. 'I can't let you alone,' he added thickly, and
Antonia's heart pounded heavily in her chest. 'Must
you go to work? I'd like to stay here all day.'

'I—must,' she averred unsteadily, forcing herself to
move out of his arms, and scurrying into the bathroom
before he came after her. 'P-put the kettle on, will you?
If you know how.'

By the time she had had a swift shower, Reed had left
the bedroom, and when she emerged with the towel
wrapped around her, she was able to dress without
interruption. The navy blue suit and cream blouse were
blessedly normal, and sobering, and when she left the
bedroom in search of her houseguest, she felt more
prepared to face the world.

She found Reed in the kitchen. He had put on her
pink towelling bathrobe, and although it was short in
the arms, its generous folds meant he was decently
covered. Its hem also exposed the hair-covered length of
his legs, but apart from the incongruity of the colour, it
did not look too outrageous.

'Tea or coffee?' he enquired, hearing the tap of her
heels and glancing up from the filter he was filling. His
eyes softened as they surveyed her neat appearance and
he gave a rueful smile. 'All present and correct, I see.'

Antonia sighed. 'Reed—you ought to be going.'

'I've made some toast, too,' he remarked, ignoring
her observation. 'Just to prove I'm capable. You can
eat some while I go and put on my clothes.' He ran an
exploring hand over the roughness of his beard. 'I don't
suppose you have a razor, do you?'

'No. And I don't want any toast either,' retorted
Antonia stiffly, as the reality of what she had allowed to
happen swept debilitatingly over her. In the morning
light, she could no longer hide from the scornful
condemnation of her conscience, and she despised
herself utterly for giving in to his persuasion.

'Okay.' Reed was regarding her thoughtfully now, as
if assessing her mood, and with a shrug he sauntered
towards her. 'I'll get dressed anyway,' he remarked, as

she stepped out of his way. 'Then I'll run you to the institute.'

'No.' Antonia swallowed. 'No, there's no need. I can get a bus.'

'Why should you get a bus, when I can take you?' enquired Reed tautly, his voice taking on a sharper edge, and she held up her head.

'Because I have no intention of walking out of here with you,' she responded, her nails digging into her palms. 'You may have no morals. I do. You can leave when you like. I'm going now.'

'Antonia!'

His mouth compressed angrily, but snatching up her handbag, she made it to the door. 'Please be gone when I get home,' she told him huskily, grasping the handle, and she let herself out without a backward glance.

The internal phone rang as Reed was putting the papers he would need in his briefcase. For a moment, his nerves tensed, as the possibility that it might be Antonia occurred to him. But then, remembering the way she had departed that morning, he dismissed the idea. If he had believed she would listen to reason, he would have met her from work that afternoon. As it was, he had this trip to New York to contend with, just when he was needing time to think, and the knowledge that Antonia would have to wait until he got back was something he was finding hard to deal with.

Picking up the receiver, he said: 'Yes?' without much enthusiasm, and then sighed when his fiancée's voice came on the line.

'Darling: I'm downstairs,' Celia exclaimed breathily. 'I know it's late, but I had to come and apologise. Press the button, won't you, darling. I'm waiting to come up.'

Reed made some positive response, and then pressed the switch which would allow the lift to come up to the twenty-second floor. While it made its swift ascent, he closed his briefcase and left his study, opening the door to his apartment as the lift reached its destination.

'Darling!' Celia emerged in a cloud of French

perfume, the hem of her mink coat brushing his legs as she reached up to bestow a warm kiss on his mouth. 'Oh, darling, I'm so sorry I wasn't home last evening as I promised. But I've had the most fantastic time in Paris!'

Reed forced a faint smile to his lips as she swept by him into the apartment, not pausing until she reached the centre of his living room. Then, slipping her arms out of her coat, she dropped it carelessly on to the sofa, and wrapped her arms around herself as Reed followed her into the room.

'I know you must be mad at me,' she exclaimed, before he could say anything. 'When I got home an hour ago, Mrs Francis couldn't *wait* to tell me you'd spent the night at the apartment, waiting for me. But— well, it was just impossible for me to get away yesterday. There was this reception yesterday evening, and Ra—I mean, the *buyers*—all stayed on for it.'

Reed expelled his breath levelly, and thrust his hands into the hip pockets of his trousers, wondering why he hadn't caught the night flight to New York after all. 'You enjoyed yourself, I gather.'

'Oh, *tremendously*!' Celia declared fervently. 'It was great fun! I don't know why I've never gone before.'

Reed nodded. 'Well—good.'

Celia sighed. 'And what about you?' she asked, contritely, slipping her hand through his arm and pressing herself against him. 'I suppose you've had a *rotten* weekend! Did you go to Stonor? But, of course you must have done.'

'Yes.' Reed detached himself without haste, and walked casually over to the drinks tray. 'Do you want a Martini?'

'Pernod, darling, please,' said Celia, subsiding on to a sofa. 'That's what I've been drinking all weekend. Lots and lots of Pernod!'

Reed poured himself a scotch, and than handed Celia her drink. '*A votre santé!*' she toasted him smilingly, lifting her glass, and Reed made some suitable comment before raising his glass to his lips.

Seating himself on the sofa opposite, he made a concerted effort to think of something relevant to say. But the headache he had had earlier in the day had returned to throb at his temples, and it was incredibly difficult to be civil to Celia when his mind was occupied elsewhere.

'So,' she said encouragingly at last, 'what sort of a weekend did you have?'

'Oh—fine.' Reed's cheeks hollowed. 'A rural one.'

'And you spent last night at the apartment,' Celia remarked, returning to her original theme. 'I'd have phoned if I'd known where you were. But I rang Stonor and I rang here, and as you weren't at either . . .' She shrugged. 'I forgot Liz was spending the weekend at her mother's.'

'It doesn't matter.' Reed wondered how he would have explained the fact of his not answering the phone if Celia had rung her apartment. *God,* he thought angrily, he should be feeling one hell of a heel, instead of tearing himself to pieces over a woman who didn't seem to care if she never saw him again!

'Is something wrong?' Not noticeably perceptive, Celia had nevertheless observed the signs of strain in Reed's face, and leaving her seat, she joined him on the sofa where he was sitting. Putting an arm around his shoulders, she rested her cheek against his sleeve, and murmured softly: 'Honestly, I'm sorry about last night. But—well, you might as well know, there was this gorgeous Frenchman, who seemed to find me quite irresistible! I was flattered. I admit it. And that's really why I stayed on. Oh—it was nothing serious. Just a— flirtation. His name was Raoul, and I let him take me to dinner. But that's all.'

Reed turned his head to look at her. 'Were you attracted to him?' he enquired tensely, and Celia shrugged.

'I suppose so.'

'How attracted?'

'Darling, not as attracted as I am to you,' she assured him firmly. 'It was just a—a weekend's flirtation. I told you. You don't have to worry. I wasn't unfaithful, or anything like that.'

Stifling an oath, Reed got to his feet, and swallowing the remainder of his drink, he went to pour himself another. The appalling truth was, he had wanted Celia to tell him she had been unfaithful. Maybe then, he could have excused his own selfish behaviour. With the knowledge that what he was doing was not so outrageous, he might have come to terms with it. As it was, his attraction to Antonia continued to torment him, like an uncontrollable fever in his blood.

'Reed—*darling*——' Celia was behind him suddenly, sliding her arms around his waist, pressing her face into the hollow of his back. 'You're not jealous, are you? You know you have no need to be.'

'I am not jealous!' Reed said the words between his teeth, wishing with an urgency that bordered on desperation that he were. 'Celia, please,' he exclaimed, extricating himself from her hands. 'Look—I've got to tell you, I'm leaving for New York in the morning. I'm sorry, but it's unavoidable. I don't know when I'll be back.'

'New York!' Celia gazed at him petulantly. 'You're not serious! You know it's Daddy's birthday on Wednesday. What about the dinner party? You promised you'd come!'

'I'm sorry.' This exchange was not going at all well, and Reed knew he was to blame. 'Something's come up, quite unexpectedly. And I've got to go myself. I promised my father I would.'

'And of course a promise to your father is more important than a promise to mine,' declared Celia sulkily.

'Cee, it's only your father's birthday. This is important!'

'My father's birthday is important,' retorted Celia sniffing. 'For heaven's sake, why can't you send someone else? Mark Hammond, perhaps. Or Lucas Turner. You always said you could delegate.'

'Not in this instance,' replied Reed flatly. 'I've got to

attend a meeting of financiers. It's not something I can
delegate.' He paused, and then said quietly: 'You can
come with me, if you like.'

'No, thank you.' Celia shook her head. 'I don't like
New York at the best of times, and *I* have no intention
of disappointing Daddy.'

'Of course.' Reed inclined his head, despising the
relief that had enveloped him at her words. If he had
thought she might have accepted, he would not have
made the offer, he realised disgustedly. Dear God, what
had Antonia done to him? Why couldn't he put her out
of his head?

'Oh, well——' Celia, as if sensing his uncertain
mood, gave a characteristic sigh. 'There's no point in
getting angry, I suppose. You have your work, and I
have mine.' She took a breath, and then continued
carefully: 'So—you won't object if I don't stay the
night, will you? I am—*rather* tired. It's been a hectic
weekend.'

Reed, who had been trying to find a reason to make
the same excuse, breathed a little more freely. 'I think
that's a good idea,' he averred swiftly. 'I've got to leave
for the airport early in the morning, and you wouldn't
want to eat breakfast alone, would you?'

Celia hesitated, his abrupt acceptance of what had
been a tentative suggestion evidently not meeting with
her approval. 'I—can stay, if you want me to,' she
ventured, but Reed was already lifting her coat from its
resting place.

'Not tonight, Cee,' he said evenly, as she rose
reluctantly to her feet. 'I'll ring you from New York
tomorrow. By the time I get back, maybe we'll both
have more time for one another.'

CHAPTER NINE

By Friday, Antonia's nerves were in a terrible state.

It had been a nervewracking week, not helped by the knowledge that once again she had allowed a man to make a fool of her. She must have been crazy to allow Reed to spend the night at the flat, she told herself fiercely. Crazier still, to go to bed with him without taking any precautions to protect herself. What if she became pregnant again? she thought desperately. What if history was to repeat itself? There was no possible chance that Reed would feel responsible for her. He had got what he wanted, and she doubted she would ever see him again.

It was all so stupid, so *ludicrous*! She had suspected what manner of man he was when he started pursuing her, but instead of sticking to her guns and keeping him at arm's length, she had allowed him to get under her skin. He had used every trick in the book to persuade her—his beautiful apartment, the house at Stonor's End; he had even pretended he cared about her daughter, when all he had really wanted to do was sleep with her. And how he had; and it was over; and she didn't know how she was going to cope with it.

She had thought, at first, that that was what she wanted. When Tuesday and Wednesday went by and he didn't ring, she had managed to convince herself that she was glad it was over. Their relationship had never had any future, she had known that, and in spite of the bitterness his betrayal aroused, she had half-believed she was unscathed by the experience.

But when Thursday came, and then Friday, and she was forced to face the fact that their brief affair really was over, the whole weight of what it meant to her enveloped her like a shroud. It was no use pretending to herself any longer. She was not—she had never been—

the kind of girl who slept around. With Simon, it could
be excused as a youthful indiscretion, an indiscretion
she had paid for with the destruction of her career.
With Reed, there were no excuses of that kind. She was
a woman now, not a child, and she could not console
herself with childish vindications. She knew why she
had let Reed stay at the flat; she knew why she had
made love with him. It was very simple: she had fallen
in love with him. In spite of herself, she had fallen
under his spell, and no amount of self-condemnation
would make it otherwise.

Of course, it was crazy. Even without his so-suitable
fiancée, he was not the kind of man to get seriously
involved with someone like her. The gulf between them
was too wide, both financially and socially. She had
been a diversion, that's all. Something he had wanted,
and got. And the guilt she had felt about Celia, and
which was now absolved, was no compensation for the
rawness his abandonment had created.

'You don't seem well,' said Mr Fenwick, on Friday
afternoon, coming into Antonia's office as she was
clearing her desk. 'Are you going north this weekend? If
not, my recommendation is that you take it easy over
the next couple of days.'

Antonia's smile was thin. 'I'm—not—going north
this weekend,' she assured him quietly. 'And I shall
probably take your advice. I am feeling a bit—under
the weather.'

'I knew it.' Mr Fenwick seemed pleased with his
diagnosis. 'I said to Heather on Wednesday that you
seemed out of sorts.'

'I'm sure it's nothing,' said Antonia, sliding her
blotter into a drawer. 'I—if that's all for today, I'll go
now. I've got some shopping to do on my way home.'

'Of course, of course.'

Mr Fenwick stepped back politely, and Antonia
slung her jacket about her shoulders. 'See you on
Monday,' she said, striving for a bright tone, and her
boss nodded understandingly as she disappeared out of
the door.

The idea of buying food was not appealing to her, but realising she had to eat if she wanted to survive this present disaster, she bought some cooked ham for her dinner. A loaf of bread and some cheese completed her purchases, and deciding to leave the bulk of her shopping until the following day, she made her way to the bus-stop. She could have walked, she supposed, feeling in her pocket for some change. The truth was, she didn't feel as if she had the energy, and she propped herself against the post, hoping she would not have to wait long.

The sleek bonnet of the Lamborghini pulling alongside her brought her up with a start, and her mouth went dry when Reed opened the window and said harshly: 'Get in!'

With a red double-decker bus looming in the distance, and Reed parked in the space where the bus would stop, Antonia did not stop to consider her actions. Pulling open the door, she scrambled into the low vehicle, and Reed drove swiftly away without saying another word.

She thought he would take her home, but he passed the turning for Clifton Gate and drove on through Maida Vale and Kilburn. He seemed to be following the signs for the North Circular Road, she thought blankly, and then abandoned that thought when he turned into the grounds of a small hotel.

Switching off the engine, he half-turned in his seat towards her, but Antonia purposely stared straight ahead. She had no idea why he had come to find her. She could not comprehend what his motives might be. And in spite of his compulsive attraction, she refused to give in to his sexual bribery.

'Are you hungry?' he inquired, evidently noticing the loaf of bread sticking out of her bag, and she shrugged.

'It—it's just some ham and cheese, for—for my dinner,' she replied unevenly.

'Are you mad at me?' he asked softly. 'You didn't seriously think we wouldn't see one another again, did you?'

Antonia shook her head. 'I don't have to think, do I?' she said, in a tense little voice. 'Only—only obey.'

'Oh, for Christ's sake!' With a smothered oath, he moved, his hand sliding possessively beneath her hair, forcing her to look at him. 'What do you take me for, you stupid little bitch?' he demanded savagely. 'I've been in New York. I just flew back this morning. I thought it would give us a breathing space, but damn it, I didn't intend it should fuel that goddamned pride of yours!'

Antonia stared at him. 'New York?' she echoed faintly, and he nodded.

'I had to attend a conference. My father arranged it all. I arrived home this morning; I took a shower, a couple of hours rest, and then I came to meet you. Unfortunately, you had left by the time I arrived.'

Antonia moistened her lips. 'I left early——'

'So your superior told me.'

'You—you spoke to Mr Fenwick?' Antonia was appalled.

'An old guy with a weight problem?' Reed's fingers gentled at her nape, and his eyes softened. 'Hell—have I missed you!'

Antonia drew back. 'Reed——'

'Shut up, will you?' he muttered, without aggression, and before she could protest, his mouth had covered hers.

The console was an irresistible barrier between them, and Reed swore again when she succeeded in using it to her advantage. 'Wh-what excuse did you give Celia for leaving your car outside Eaton Lodge all night?' she got out huskily, deliberately raising his fiancée's name between them, and Reed regarded her broodingly before flinging himself back in his seat.

'I didn't have to give her an excuse,' he retorted harshly. 'She didn't arrive back from Paris until Monday, and Mrs Francis assumed I had spent the night in the apartment upstairs.'

'I see.' Antonia swallowed. 'How convenient!'

'Yes. Wasn't it?' Reed's nostrils flared. 'I'm lucky that way.'

'So—where are you going now?' Antonia enquired carefully. 'To—to see Celia?'

Reed expelled his breath wearily. 'Is that likely?' he demanded. 'As a matter of fact, Cee doesn't even know I'm back in the country. So far as she's concerned, I'm still in the big apple! Does that satisfy you?'

Antonia bent her head. 'So where are you going?'

'I thought—I really thought—we might be driving north,' declared Reed quietly. 'But as you're buying ham and cheese for your evening meal, I guess you haven't any plans for that.'

Antonia gasped. 'You really expected to go to Newcastle?'

'To meet Susie? Yes, why not?'

'After—after what happened?'

'Particularly after what happened,' he retorted roughly. 'Oh, Toni——' it was the first time he had abbreviated her name, except when he was making love to her, and her senses tingled; '—I don't want to forget what happened!' He gazed at her intently, his eyes sensually brilliant. 'I want to do it again! Over and over. Until you can't think or feel or *taste* anyone else but me!'

'You're crazy——'

'About you? Yes, I am,' he conceded emotively. 'Let's go to Newcastle, Antonia. Let's spend the weekend together, at least. Hell, I'll even promise to be good, if you'll just stop fighting me!'

Antonia bent her head. 'We can't——'

'Why can't we?'

'I haven't packed, and we can't go to the flat——'

'Buy a toothbrush,' declared Reed reasonably. 'What else?'

'I haven't told my mother.'

'Phone her.'

'Wh-what can I say?'

'Tell her a friend has offered to drive you up for the weekend, and you don't want to refuse.'

Aware that she was allowing him to railroad her again, Antonia shook her head. 'I can't.'

'Why the hell not?'

Antonia gulped. 'Because you don't care, do you? You don't care about anyone but yourself. So long as you get your own way, you don't give a damn!'

Reed hunched his shoulders, and for several moments there was silence in the car. Then, flatly, he conceded her accusation: 'No,' he said, flexing his neck muscles with weary impatience. 'No, you're right. I'm completely amoral.' He reached for the ignition. 'I'll take you home. I can always tell Cee I gave you a lift from the bus-stop.'

Antonia, who had been expecting another argument, felt her stomach plunge as he spoke. His careless acknowledgment of her words left her with a distinctly hollow feeling inside her, and although she knew if she remained silent he would do as he had promised, her treacherous emotions refused to let it go.

'It's easy for you, isn't it?' she choked bitterly, as the engine sprang to life. 'Off with a mistress, and on with a fiancée! Either way, you can't lose!'

'Is that what you think?' His lips twisted as he looked at her.

'It's the truth! You—you satisfy your—your carnal desires with—with one or other of us, don't you?'

Reed swore then, an ugly word that Antonia could not mistake, and the engine died as he grasped her face between his hands. 'Do you really want to know the truth?' he snarled, and she trembled at the anger in his expression. 'The truth is—I haven't been able to *touch* Cee since that night I took you to the apartment! You say it's easy for me—well, believe me, it's not!' His incensed breath filled her mouth and she tried to look away from him, but he would not let her. 'Let me tell you,' he went on grimly, 'I didn't intend to get involved with you. God help me, I thought I felt sorry for you! I fooled myself into thinking we could be friends! *Friends!*' He groaned. 'Friends don't fill your mind to the exclusion of everything—and everyone—else! Friends don't keep you awake half the night, with the kind of ache I haven't had since I was a schoolboy!' His eyes darkened. 'It dawned on me by degrees, that what I really wanted to do was make love with you, and that's a complication I could have done without!'

Antonia shivered. 'I didn't ask you to——'

'Goddammit, I know that!' he grated heavily, his fingers sliding into her hair. 'But you have to know the way it is!' He expelled an unsteady breath. 'Now—do I take you back to the flat?'

Antonia moved her head helplessly from side to side. 'Oh, Reed! What can I say?'

'You can tell the truth,' he declared huskily, tipping her face up to his. 'You don't want to leave me, any more than I want to leave you. Am I right?'

Antonia closed her eyes against the possessive passion in his and then, slowly, nodded her head. 'I'll phone my mother,' she agreed unevenly, and the searching pressure of his mouth on her parted lips sealed her guilty submission.

Mrs Lord was very surprised to hear that her daughter was phoning from a motorway service area. 'But, who is this man you're bringing home for the weekend?' she protested blankly. 'You've never mentioned him before. Have you known him long? Does he work at the institute?'

'I suppose I've known him nearly a month,' replied Antonia uncomfortably. 'And no—he doesn't work at the institute.'

'Well, what does he do then? And where did you meet him?' Mrs Lord sounded a little impatient now. 'Antonia, you have to be a little more forthcoming. I mean, what do you know about him? Are you sure you want to bring him here? What about Susie?'

'He's quite respectable, Mum,' exclaimed Antonia, half-humorously. 'Honestly, you'll like him.'

'But what does he do?'

Antonia hesitated. 'He—he's a businessman. He owns a company.'

'*Owns?*' Mrs Lord sounded impressed. 'Well, I must say, he sounds an improvement on Simon Sheldon!'

'It's nothing like that, Mum.' Antonia's tone sharpened. 'We're just—friends. That's all.'

'So why are you bringing him here?' demanded Mrs Lord impatiently.

'To—to meet Susie,' replied Antonia swiftly. 'I must go, Mum. My coins are running out.'

'Wait a minute!' Her mother was not quite finished, and reluctantly, Antonia pushed another coin into the meter. 'Have you forgotten it's my bridge night? I mean, I put it off the night you came home, but you haven't given me any warning this time.'

'That's okay, Mum.' Antonia was quite relieved that Mrs Lord would not be there when they first arrived. 'Lucy's baby-sitting, isn't she? Just tell her we should arrive about ten o'clock.'

Reed was waiting for her in the restaurant, a lean attractive figure in his dark corded trousers and black leather jerkin. 'Did you get through?' he enquired, re-seating himself after she had taken her place opposite, and Antonia swallowed a mouthful of the wine he had ordered for her before nodding vigorously.

'It's her bridge night,' she said, glancing nervously about her. 'Aren't you afraid someone might recognise you? You're not exactly unremarkable!'

'Thank you.' Reed's tone was sardonic. 'But right now, I don't particularly care.' He covered her hand with his and slid his thumb into her palm. 'What are you going to eat?'

Antonia's pulses raced. 'Wh-what are you?' she asked a little breathily, and for a few moments they were absorbed with a consultation over the menu.

But when the waitress had taken their order, and they were alone again, Reed said quietly: 'Tell me about Sheldon: your ex-husband. I want to know about him.'

Antonia lifted her shoulders. 'There's nothing to tell.'

'Don't give me that.' Reed regarded her intently across the lamplit table. 'Why did you marry him? Did you love him? Where is he now? I want to know.'

Antonia bent her head. 'I married him because I was pregnant,' she admitted softly, her cheeks flaming as she felt his gaze upon her. 'I was nineteen. He was twenty-one.'

'Go on.'

She quivered, and drew her hands together in her lap. 'What more is there to say? I had been at university for a year, and I was still a virgin.' She grimaced. 'All my friends thought that I was an anathema. Then, in the summer holidays, Simon started taking me out. He was very popular, and I was very naive. Does that answer your question?'

Reed sighed. 'Did you love him?'

'I thought I did. But—well, after—after *it* happened, I didn't want to see him again.'

'Why not?'

'Oh, Reed!' She shook her head. 'Don't make me have to spell it out.'

'Okay.' Reed's tone was gentle. 'So when you discovered you were going to have a baby, you panicked.'

'My mother did,' conceded Antonia ruefully. 'And—and my father was sick, and I didn't want to hurt anyone . . .' She shrugged. 'It was a long time ago.'

'So you got married.' Reed was implacable, and she sighed.

'Yes, yes. We got married. My parents gave us enough to put down a deposit on a small house and Simon's job at the electronic's factory gave him plenty of scope for overtime.'

'So, what went wrong?'

Antonia turned her head away. 'We—weren't—compatible.'

'You mean he met someone else.'

'Several someones,' admitted Antonia unhappily. 'It was my fault, I suppose. I never did measure up to his expectations of me.'

'What's that supposed to mean?'

'Reed, stop it! I can't talk to you about these things.'

'Why not?'

'Because they're personal.'

Reed regarded her averted face for several seconds,

and then he said softly: 'I guess he accused you of being frigid, hmm?'

Antonia's lips parted and her eyes turned bewilderedly to his. 'How did you know? Am I?'

Reed's laughter was reassuringly intimate. 'Oh, love, you know the answer to that, without me having to tell you,' he answered huskily.

'Then——?'

'It's the usual excuse for a man's inadequacy,' he responded, meeting her anxious gaze. 'Okay, okay. Just one more question. Where is he now?'

'I'm not sure.' Antonia looked doubtful. 'After— after we split up, he left Newcastle. I heard he had joined the Navy, but I'm not sure. He never writes. He never kept in touch at all. I doubt if Susie even remembers him.'

Reed inclined his head. 'I can't say I'm sorry.'

'No.' Antonia allowed a small smile to touch her lips. 'Nor am I.'

When dinner was over, Antonia went into the service shop and bought herself a toothbrush. At least her mother would not be around to observe she had brought no luggage, she reflected thankfully. And she had some old clothes at home she could wear instead of the navy suit.

Sliding into the Lamborghini again, Antonia felt a momentary pang for the ease with which she had accepted this arrangement. The trouble was, she always felt at ease with Reed, and it was this, more than anything else, that warned her to fight his dark attraction. It would be too easy to give in, to be grateful for whatever crumbs of his time he might throw in her direction. She had to always remember he was going to marry someone else, and that no matter how attracted he might be to her, it was Celia Lytton-Smythe who was going to become *Mrs* Reed Gallagher.

To her relief, Reed didn't ask her any more questions, and pretty soon the mesmeric sameness of the motorway uncoiling ahead of them caused her eyelids to droop. She tried to keep awake, chivvying herself with the guilty awareness that Reed, and not she, should be tired. But it was no use. The unhappy week she had spent, worrying over her feelings for the man beside her, had caused many restless nights, and almost without her being aware of it, she drowsed the journey away.

Reed aroused her as they were driving through the outskirts of the city, his rueful smile mirroring his regret at having to do so. 'Which way?' he asked, as they crossed the massive arch of the Tyne Bridge, and Antonia struggled up in her seat to give him hasty directions.

It was only a quarter-to-ten when the Lamborghini turned into the cul-de-sac and Antonia's nerves tightened as Reed drove the short distance to her mother's comfortable semi-detached. Now that she was here, she was intensely conscious of how he might react to his surroundings, and like the first time he came to the flat, she was painfully defensive of her home.

'Do you want me to leave the car on the road?' he asked surveying the short drive to the garage, and Antonia frowned.

'Well—perhaps for the present,' she conceded, wondering who else had observed their arrival. 'My mother's out this evening, and she'll want to put her car away when she gets home. After that, you could park it on the drive.'

'All right.' Reed gave her a wry smile and thrust open his door. 'You think she'll let me stay then?'

Antonia avoided his eyes. 'You're here, aren't you?' she responded, following his example and opening her door. 'Come on. Susie's baby-sitter is expecting us.'

Reed had removed his jacket for driving, but now he looped it over one shoulder to follow her up the path. With his tie pulled a couple of inches away from his collar, and the top two buttons of his dark green shirt unfastened, he looked devastatingly attractive, and Antonia couldn't altogether blame Lucy Telfer for the wide-eyed admiration that followed her opening of the door.

'Hello Antonia,' she said, stepping back to allow them to enter the hall. At sixteen, Lucy was far more experienced than Antonia had been at that age, and she was making no secret of the fact that she found Reed absolutely fascinating. 'Your mother told me you were coming. Did you have a good journey?'

All this was said with her eyes firmly glued to Reed's vaguely amused face, and Antonia found her patience growing increasingly thin. 'It was a very pleasant journey, thank you,' she said, annoyed to hear the edge in her voice. 'I—Reed, this is Lucy. She lives next door.'

'Hello Lucy.' As usual, Reed was completely at ease with his surroundings. 'Is it okay if I hang this here?'

As if he was a regular visitor to the house, Reed draped his jacket over the banister before following the two girls into a comfortable living room. An open fire was burning in the grate, for although the house was centrally heated, Mrs Lord liked the living flame, and a television was playing in one corner. Evidence of Lucy's occupation was there in the glossy magazines residing on the couch, and the remains of the supper Mrs Lord had left for her rested on a tray.

'I'll clear up,' said Antonia shortly, as Lucy would have picked up her tray, and the younger girl grimaced.

'If you're sure,' she murmured, her eyes on Reed again as he stood gazing at the television, and Antonia took off her jacket and dropped it on to a chair.

'I'm sure,' she said, waiting impatiently for Lucy to collect her belongings. 'And—thanks. For baby-sitting, I mean.'

'That's all right.' Lucy was offhand, sensing the older woman's desire to be rid of her and resenting it. She turned to Reed and smiled. 'I might see you again tomorrow—er—Reed,' she murmured, tilting her head provocatively, and Reed dragged his attention from the television to make a polite assention.

Antonia saw her to the door and then came tensely back to the living room. In her absence, Reed had not moved his position, but as she came through the door, he came towards her.

'You don't have to be, you know,' he said roughly, his hands sliding possessively over her shoulders, and she gazed uncomprehendingly up at him. 'Jealous,' he added flatly, resisting her attempts to break away from him. 'You were, weren't you? Dear God, what do you take me for?'

Antonia shook her head, and then with a little moan, she allowed him to pull her closer. Pressing her face against the taut expanse of his chest, warm beneath the fine material of his shirt, she breathed deeply of his clean male smell, filling her nostrils with the scent of him, as his muscled body filled her mind to the exclusion of all else.

'Do you know what you're doing?' he demanded, against her mouth, his hands at her hips making her overwhelmingly aware of his arousal, and with a supreme effort, she broke free of him.

'I—I must tidy up,' she said unsteadily, going towards the tray, and with a groan of impatience, Reed went after her.

It was as well they had their backs to the door, Antonia thought later, remembering the sensuous feel of Reed's palms against her nipples. He was in the process of unbuttoning her blouse to facilitate the invasion of his hands when Antonia heard her daughter's voice, but he released her almost immediately when Susie sidled into the room.

'Mummy?' she said doubtfully, coming round the couch towards them, and Antonia just had time to straighten her clothes before the little girl saw her. 'Oh, Mummy!' she exclaimed, abandoning her uncertainty and rushing into Antonia's arms. 'Nanna didn't tell me you were coming!'

'Nanna didn't know,' Antonia assured her gently, smoothing the silky dark hair out of Susie's eyes and giving her a breathtaking hug. 'I didn't know myself until this afternoon. I—Mr Gallagher very kindly offered me a lift.'

Susie drew away from her mother sufficiently to look up at Reed, standing silently beside them, and her small face grew serious. 'Are you Mr Galla—Gallagher?' she asked, stumbling a little over the word, and Reed came down on his haunches so that she could better see his face.

'Reed,' he amended gently, his lean face creasing into a smile. 'So long as I can call you Susie, of course, and not Miss Sheldon.'

Susie's chin dimpled. 'Nobody calls me *Miss* Sheldon,' she exclaimed, glancing at her mother for support. 'Can I really call you Reed?'

'Do you want to?'

Susie nodded.

'Reed it is, then,' he assured her equably, and Antonia realised he had disarmed the child without her even being aware of it.

'Do you have a car?' Susie asked now, as her mother straightened, and Antonia endeavoured to recover her composure.

'Not tonight, Susie,' she said, pointing firmly at the clock. 'You should be in bed and asleep, not creeping down the stairs and asking questions.'

'Oh, but—*Reed* won't be here tomorrow,' protested the little girl disappointedly, and Antonia drew a breath.

'Yes, he will,' she said levelly. 'He's going to spend the weekend with us. And——' She paused and glanced at Reed, who had now got to his feet again. 'He'll tell you all about his car tomorrow.'

'And give you a ride, too, if you'd like one,' agreed Reed irrepressibly. 'You and your Mummy both. How about that?'

'Really? Tomorrow?' Susie was excited. 'You're sleeping at my house?'

'If your Mummy can find me a bed,' remarked Reed drily, causing Antonia's colour to rise once again. 'Is that all right?'

Susie clasped her hands together. 'I'll never sleep, you know. I don't; not when something exciting's going to happen.'

'Then you'll have to lie awake,' declared Antonia,

reasonably, putting a teasing finger on her daughter's nose. 'Now—say good night to—to Reed. You'll see him again in the morning.'

Susie was loathe to settle down, but the anticipation of the promised outing the following day eventually persuaded her to behave herself. 'He's nice, isn't he, Mummy?' she murmured, as Antonia tucked the covers around her. 'Reed, I mean. Are you going to marry him?'

'Marry him?' Antonia was appalled. 'Don't be silly, Sue!'

'I'm not being silly.' Susie pouted. 'Auntie Sylvia said it was time you thought about getting married again. She said it isn't fair to—to expect Nanna to look after me all the time.'

'Well, there's no chance of me marrying Mr Gallagher,' declared Antonia brusquely, resenting her sister-in-law's careless tongue. 'Go to sleep, darling. We can talk again tomorrow. And don't get up when Nanna comes home, or she won't be very pleased.'

Downstairs again, Antonia found that Reed had discovered the whereabouts of the kitchen for himself, and was presently disposing of Lucy's leftovers into the waste bin. 'You see, I'm quite domesticated,' he remarked, grinning at her surprised face. 'It's what comes of an Irish upbringing. Sure, and didn't I milk the cows and collect the eggs before I was old enough to go to school!'

'You're incorrigible,' she exclaimed, shaking her head, and he dried his hands and came to meet her.

'And you're beautiful,' he told her, burying his face in the hollow at her nape. 'How soon will your mother be back? Or is that a leading question?'

'Any minute now,' said Antonia unsteadily, her bones melting at the sensuous brush of his tongue, and as if to confirm the truth of her statement, she heard the distinctive sound of her mother's key in the lock.

By the time her mother had come into the hall, Antonia and Reed were standing in the doorway to the living room, and Mrs Lord met her daughter's gaze only briefly before transferring her attention to her companion.

'Mr—Gallagher, isn't it?' she observed, not waiting for Antonia's introduction, but coming forward with her hand outstretched. 'I'm Antonia's mother, Mrs Lord. I hope she's made you welcome to our home.'

'I'm delighted to be here, and to meet you, Mrs Lord,' replied Reed gallantly, as Antonia caught her breath. 'And please—my name's Reed. When I'm called Mr Gallagher, I always feel as though my father should be here.'

Mrs Lord smiled, evidently liking his easy courtesy. 'Have you been here long?' she enquired, as Antonia came to bestow a warm kiss on her cheek. 'Where's Lucy? I hope you've sent her home.'

'We have,' said Antonia, taking her mother's coat and hanging it away in the cloakroom. 'Did you have a nice evening?'

'I lost, if that's what you mean,' remarked Mrs Lord drily, passing them to enter the living room. 'Make some coffee, will you, Antonia? I'm sure—Reed could drink a cup.'

Antonia was reluctant to leave Reed alone with her mother, but she had little choice. She guessed Mrs Lord had engineered this to speak with him without her daughter's presence, and stifling her unease, Antonia hurried back into the kitchen.

She need not have been concerned. When she returned some fifteen minutes later with the tray of coffee and biscuits, she found Mrs Lord and Reed talking easily together, and her fears seemed totally groundless when she met her mother's innocent gaze. Ensconced in her favourite position on the sofa, with Reed sprawled in the armchair opposite, Mrs Lord was evidently enjoying herself, and Antonia wondered how Reed had explained his friendship with her daughter.

Reed rose at Antonia's entrance, and set the low coffee table near the sofa so that she could deposit the tray. Then, he accepted the cup she prepared for him, seeming not to notice the anxious look she cast towards him.

'Reed was just telling me he's met Susie already,' remarked Mrs Lord, as Antonia subsided on to the sofa beside her. 'Little minx! I purposely didn't tell her who had phoned, so she would behave herself.'

'I expect she heard our voices,' said Reed lazily, putting his cup aside, and Antonia wondered if he would have preferred something stronger.

'I expect she did,' agreed Mrs Lord, helping herself to a square of shortbread. 'She so looks forward to her mother's visits. It's a pity Antonia has to work so far away. I'm sure you'll agree, a child needs her mother.'

'Mum!' Antonia gave her mother a speaking look. 'Reed's not interested in our . . . *personal* problems.'

'Isn't he?' Mrs Lord seemed unrepentant, and Antonia's face burned. 'I'm sure—Reed—understands the difficulties of the present economic situation better than we do. As an employer, he must have faced the problem dozens of times.'

'It's a pity Susie can't live with her mother,' commented Reed, and Antonia turned frustrated eyes in his direction. 'Although, I have to say,' he added evenly, 'London is not a place to bring up children; not if there's an alternative.'

'Do you live in London, Reed?' enquired Mrs Lord innocently, and her daughter wanted to die of embarrassment.

'I have an apartment in town, yes,' he responded, without resentment. 'But I also own a house in Oxfordshire, and I try to spend as much time as I can there.'

'In Oxfordshire!' remarked Mrs Lord with interest. 'How lovely! My husband and I spent a holiday there once. We stayed at Woodstock. Do you know it?'

'I've been there,' conceded Reed, after a moment. 'I hope to spend more time exploring the area in the future.'

'You're not from that area then?' probed Mrs Lord persistently, and Antonia caught her breath.

'Mum, what is this? An inquisition?' She sighed impatiently. 'I think perhaps I should show our guest to

his room, don't you? He just got back from the United
States this morning, and I'm sure he must be tired.'

'A business trip?' suggested Mrs Lord irrepressibly,
as Antonia got purposefully to her feet, and Reed
smiled.

'In a manner of speaking,' he replied, following
Antonia's example. And then, with innate politeness, he
added: 'It's very kind of you to allow me to stay here,
Mrs Lord. I do appreciate it.'

'It's our pleasure,' responded Antonia's mother
charmingly. 'I've put Reed in Howard's old room,
Antonia. I think he'll be comfortable there.'

'Who is Howard?' murmured Reed in her ear, as they
ascended the stairs, and Antonia quivered.

'My brother,' she told him, as his lips brushed her ear.
'He—er—you may meet him tomorrow. He and his
wife sometimes come to tea on Saturdays.'

'I'll look forward to it,' declared Reed mockingly, his
hand at her waist disturbingly possessive. 'Which is
your room?' he added, as they reached the upstairs
landing.

'My room, my mother's room, Susie's room—and
yours,' Antonia pointed out softly, leading the way
across the landing to the door furthest from the stairs.
'And that's the bathroom,' she appended, indicating the
fifth door. 'I'm sorry, but you'll have to share. We
don't have two bathrooms, I'm afraid.'

'I guess I'll survive,' remarked Reed drily, following
her into her brother's old room. There were still
football pennants on the walls, and photographs of
Howard when he was a member of the school rugby
team. But the room was warm and comfortable, and in
the lamplight it did not look too shabby.

'If you're not warm enough, there are extra blankets
in the ottoman,' observed Antonia, gesturing towards
the chest at the foot of the bed. 'My mother doesn't like
duvets, so I'm afraid we're rather old-fashioned when it
comes to bedding.'

'After spending last night in a sleeper-seat, this will
be absolute luxury,' Reed assured her drily. 'Toni, stop

worrying about me. I can take care of myself.' He paused. 'And that includes handling your mother, too.'

Antonia bent her head. 'She's awfully inquisitive.'

'She's a mother,' retorted Reed, putting his hand beneath her chin and tipping it upward. 'Now—I'm going to get my case from the car, before I flake out.' He bent his head to brush her lips with his. 'Okay?'

CHAPTER TEN

ANTONIA awoke to the sound of her daughter's voice chattering away in the room next door. For a moment, she was disorientated, unable to comprehend why Susie should be in Howard's room at all. And then, she remembered who was occupying her brother's bed, and a wave of nervous apprehension swept over her.

In spite of her exhaustion, she had not slept well. She had lain awake for hours after the other occupants of the house had settled down for the night, wondering—in reality *hoping*—that Reed might come to her room. But he hadn't. By the time her mother had allowed her to come upstairs, Reed had had time to wash and undress and get into bed, and there was no sound from his room as Antonia attended to her own toilette.

But now, Susie had evidently taken it upon herself to waken their unexpected guest, and realising she could not allow her daughter to go on making a nuisance of herself, Antonia slid reluctantly out of bed. Pulling on her old woollen dressing gown, she only paused long enough to run combing fingers through her hair before hurrying next door. A proper appraisal of her appearance would depress her too much, she reflected, unaware that without make-up she looked infinitely younger, and more vulnerable.

The door of Howard's room was ajar, and not bothering to knock, Antonia pushed it wider. 'Susie!' she exclaimed reprovingly, discovering her daughter perched on the end of Reed's bed, and the little girl's face took on a rueful expression as her mother advanced into the room.

'It's all right, Toni. I don't mind,' Reed inserted gently, and Antonia was forced to look at the man reclining lazily on the pillows. The darkness of his skin was pronounced against the whiteness of the bedding, and the fine whorls of dark hair that lightly spread down to his rib-cage and beyond, brought a vivid memory of their abrasive texture against her breasts.

'I——' Her breath catching in her throat at the sexual appeal of his muscled body, Antonia shook her head. 'She—she shouldn't be here,' she said, switching her attention back to the safer features of the little girl. 'Susie, you know you don't go disturbing people at this hour of the morning! It's only half-past-seven! Heavens, Nanna isn't even up yet!'

'Reed was awake, weren't you?' protested Susie hopefully, looking to the occupant of the bed for support, and he nodded.

'That's right. I was awake,' he assured Antonia lazily. 'I'm sorry if we disturbed you. Susie was just telling me about falling off Helen's bicycle.'

Antonia pressed her lips together. 'Nevertheless——'

'Did we wake you up, Mummy?' interrupted Susie quickly. 'I've been awake for ages. Reed says he's going to take me out in his car this morning. I've seen it out of the window. It's ever so long and sneaky.'

'Susie——'

'I think perhaps you'd better get out of here, so I can get dressed,' Reed put in swiftly. He gave Susie a deliberate wink. 'We don't want to upset your mother, do we? She might not let you come out with us, if she's mad!'

Antonia gave him an indignant look, but Susie was already scrambling off the bed. 'I'll go and get dressed,' she declared, skipping past her mother. 'Can I wear my new dungarees?'

'Provided you have a thorough wash first,' replied Antonia tersely, feeling decidedly put out. 'And clean your teeth, remember?'

'Yes, Mummy.'

Susie sailed out of the door in high spirits, but when Antonia would have followed her, Reed put out his hand. 'Close the door,' he said softly, his eyes warmly indulgent, and although she knew she was being reckless, she automatically obeyed him.

'Come here,' he said, and with a feeling of helplessness she approached the bed.

'I can't stay,' she got out huskily, but Reed was already drawing her down beside him.

'You shouldn't have come then,' he told her, his hand sliding behind her nape and compelling her insistently towards him. 'Did I tell you, you're the only woman I know who looks good in the morning?'

'And you've had plenty of experience,' she breathed, as his tongue brushed her ear.

'Some,' he conceded modestly, his lips moving sensuously on hers. And then, with consummate ease, the pressure of his mouth hardened into passion, the kiss deepening and lengthening, so that when he drew her down on to the pillows, she had no will to resist. The drugging magic of his mouth was destroying all her inhibitions, and she no longer cared where they were or who might see them, so long as Reed continued his hungry assault.

Her hands slid over his chest, revelling in the feel of his hair-roughened flesh beneath her fingers, and with a little groan, he released the belt of her dressing gown, so that all that was between them was the frail barrier of her cotton nightshirt.

Turning, Reed was above her now, and dragging the covers aside, he gathered her trembling body into the bed beside him. Immediately, she was conscious of the lean strength of his legs, naked as they imprisoned hers, and the swollen pressure of his manhood hard against her stomach.

'I know, I know—we can't!' he muttered roughly, as she started to resist him, 'but just let me hold you for a few moments. Christ, it's bad enough sleeping in the room next to yours and not being able to touch you, without denying me this small pleasure!'

Antonia's fingers curled into the hair at his nape. 'I— I thought you might have——' She broke off discomfortedly, and he buried his face between her breasts.

'Did you think I didn't want to?' he demanded in a

muffled voice. 'Oh, Toni—I didn't feel as if I should. I mean, inviting myself up here; accepting your mother's hospitality. I didn't want you to think that was why I had come.'

'And wasn't it?' she breathed unsteadily, and he lifted his head.

'I wanted to spend the weekend with you,' he told her softly. 'Oh, I'm not denying I want you—really want you, I mean. Here—like this. But I do enjoy just being *with* you, and I did want to meet Susie. It wasn't just a line.'

Antonia touched his mouth with her fingertips, and his lips parted to allow them access. 'I want you, too,' she confessed, unable to hold back the words, her fingers tingling at the sensual caress of his tongue. 'I've wanted to see you all week. I hated myself for what I said to you on Monday.'

'I wish I'd known,' he muttered, lowering his head to nuzzle the peak of her breast, thrusting against the thin covering of her nightshirt. 'When I flew out of London on Tuesday morning, I had a God-awful feeling in my gut, and if I'd thought you wouldn't hang up on me, I'd have phoned you Tuesday night.'

'Oh, Reed!'

'Yes—oh, Reed!' he said thickly, and then, with a sudden change of mood, he compelled her out of the bed. 'I think you'd better go,' he told her harshly, rolling over on to his stomach. 'I can only take so much, and right now, I'm at the limit of my endurance.'

Antonia gathered up her dressing gown and wrapped it about her. 'Are you getting up?'

He glanced over his shoulder. 'Do you have a shower?'

'Yes.'

'Good.' He swung round and sat up, crossing his legs Buddha fashion. 'Can I take one?' He grimaced. 'A cold one, preferably.'

By the time Reed came downstairs, dark and handsome, in mud-coloured Levis and a matching cotton shirt, Antonia was helping her mother prepare breakfast. But her heart flipped a beat when he came into the kitchen and she met the lazy indulgence of his gaze. Dear God, she thought wildly, how was she going to exist when he married Celia? The idea of him sharing the same intimacies with another woman that they had both shared, filled her with desperation, and she tore her eyes away abruptly, wishing she had never brought him here.

'Eggs and bacon all right, Reed?' inquired Mrs Lord, as Susie, having heard his descent of the stairs, came dancing through from the living room.

'That's fine, thanks,' he responded, allowing the little girl to grab hold of his hand, and Susie giggled as she dragged him towards the door.

'Come on,' she said. 'I want to show you how to play space invaders. Nanna bought it for me for my birthday, and I bet I can get more points than you can.'

'I bet you can,' conceded Reed good-humouredly, giving Antonia a rueful grin. 'Okay, okay; I'm coming. But you must make allowances for my inexperience.'

'Susie——' began Antonia doubtfully, but her mother touched her arm.

'Leave her alone,' she advised quietly, forking curls of crispy bacon from the grill. 'Reed's very good with her. Hadn't you noticed? I'd have thought the exchange they were having earlier would have wakened the dead!'

Antonia set out knives and forks on the scrubbed pine table. 'You heard them, too?' she murmured awkwardly.

'And your intervention,' agreed Mrs Lord drily. 'You mustn't blame Susie. She's never had a man to take an interest in her before.'

'You mean a father, don't you?' remarked Antonia tautly. 'Mum, Reed and I—we're not—*serious* about one another.'

'Aren't you?' Her mother cast her a sceptical glance. 'Don't you really mean, he is, but you're not?'

Antonia gasped. 'I don't know what——'

'Yes, you do, Antonia.' Her mother sighed. 'I've seen the way you look at him. And I've seen the way he looks at you. My God, if ever a man was obsessed with a woman, Reed Gallagher is with you!'

'You're crazy!' Antonia dropped the salt cellar, and uttered an imprecation as the fine grains scattered about the floor. She sighed as she bent to sweep them up with a paper towel. 'I wish you'd stop imagining things, Mum. You hardly know the man!'

'Well—I know what I know,' retorted Mrs Lord obscurely, breaking eggs into the pan. 'Put some more bread in the toaster, will you, dear? And just remember—all men aren't like Simon Sheldon!'

After breakfast, Reed drove Antonia, and Susie, into Newcastle, to do some shopping for her mother. They parked in the multi-storey complex at Eldon Square, and then Antonia showed him round the huge shopping arcade, which was reputed to be the largest in Europe. It was easier to keep a sense of detachment in Susie's presence, and if Reed noticed Antonia's efforts to keep the child between them, he politely avoided commenting on the fact. Instead, he generously gave his time to Susie, allowing her to dictate where they went and what they did, and if Antonia's feelings had not been so traumatic, she would have appreciated the efforts he was making.

While Antonia went round the food department at Marks and Spencers, Reed suggested taking Susie into the toy department at Fenwicks, and they met up later to make their way back to the car. Susie was wearing a distinctly smug expression now, and as Reed took Antonia's bags from her, she noticed the suspicious carrier her daughter was hiding behind her back. Oh, well, she thought wearily, if Reed had bought Susie something, she could hardly object. It was his money, after all, and he wasn't likely to see her again after this weekend.

Back at home, Susie was evidently bubbling over with excitement. While Reed deposited the bags of shopping on the kitchen table, the little girl unpacked her own carrier, handing over a separate bag to her mother.

'This is for you,' she said importantly, glancing over her shoulder as Reed came back into the living room. 'It's all right if I give it to Mummy now, isn't it?' she requested. 'You did say I could, once we got back home.'

Antonia pressed her lips together. 'Reed——'

'Take it,' he said flatly. 'It's—well, call it a token of my appreciation for letting me spend the weekend here.'

With Susie looking on with anxious eyes, Antonia felt obliged to open the bag, and her lips parted incredulously as she drew out the silky object it contained. It was a dress, made of fine cashmere, so delicately woven it took up very little space. Its colour was less easy to define—a subtle blend of tawny gold and bronze, that almost exactly matched the colour of her hair. The sleeveless bodice had a deep vee neckline, and the skirt was full and gently flared. It was the most beautiful dress she had ever seen in her life, and her eyes lifted to Reed's in total confusion.

'The sales assistant was about your size,' he remarked carelessly, as the soft material spilled through her hands. 'If you don't like it, I've no doubt you can change it.'

'But you do like it, don't you, Mummy?' exclaimed Susie, breaking the spell that had gripped Antonia ever since she had opened the bag, and she bent her head, nodding a little jerkily as she did so.

'Yes. Yes, it's lovely,' she murmured, fighting back the urge to burst into tears. 'I—I don't know what to say to you.'

'Say you like it,' said Reed quietly, watching her with guarded eyes, and unable to deny it, she covered the space between them.

'I do. I do like it,' she said huskily, looking up at him. And then, gripping his hand tightly, she reached up and kissed his cheek.

Reed's fingers moved to grip hers, and she knew if Susie had not been there, he would have responded far more satisfactorily. As it was, a little of the tension eased out of his face, and forcing himself to speak naturally, he said softly: 'You could wear it tonight. When I take you out for dinner.'

'Am I going out for dinner, too?' demanded Susie, pushing herself between them, and Reed's lazy smile took away her disappointment at his response.

'Not this time,' he told her, lifting the carrier bag out of her hands and extracting the bulky object that was still inside. 'Who is going to show Garfield where he's to sleep, if you're not here to look after him?' he exclaimed, depositing the orange cat in her arms. 'You said he'd probably feel lonely, leaving all those other cats in the shop. You wouldn't go out and leave him, would you? Not on his first night in a strange bed!'

Reed had a gift for Mrs Lord, too; a small pearl brooch, which she was evidently charmed with. 'You really shouldn't,' she said, at lunch, admiring the way it glinted on her lapel. But her reaction on her return from the hairdressers had been all Reed could have wanted, and Antonia dreaded what her mother would say when she saw her dress.

As Antonia had anticipated, Howard and Sylvia and the twins came over in the afternoon. 'Your mother was so intrigued that you were bringing a man home, she couldn't wait to phone us,' declared Sylvia, as she came to find her sister-in-law in the kitchen, revealing that their visit was hardly accidental. 'But I must admit, he's not at all what I expected. However did you meet such a dishy man?'

'What did you expect, Sylvia?' enquired Antonia, setting teacups and saucers on a tray. 'He's nothing like Simon, if that's what you mean. And if my mother's made some allusion to our being—well, involved, forget it!'

'You mean, you're not—sleeping together?' probed Sylvia maliciously, and Antonia's eyes sparkled angrily.

'No, we're not,' she denied, controlling her colour with difficulty. 'And now, if you don't mind, I'll make the tea!'

There was another reason why Howard and Sylvia

had made the journey from Tynemouth to Gosforth, which became evident later in the afternoon.

'Howard's been given four tickets for tonight's performance of the play at the Royal,' his wife inserted at the first opportunity. 'It's supposed to be a very funny play, and they're awfully good seats.' She paused. 'We wondered—Howard and I, that is—whether Antonia and . . . and Reed might like to go with us.'

'How lovely!'

Mrs Lord was enthusiastic, but before Antonia could do more than exchange a helpless glance with Reed, Sylvia had something else to add.

'The only thing is,' she went on, and Antonia wondered why she found the rueful tone her sister-in-law had adopted so suspect, 'we don't have a baby-sitter; and no doubt you're looking after Susie, Mum, so it makes things a little difficult.'

Howard, noticing his sister's expression, said gallantly: 'You can have two of the tickets anyway, Antonia. I mean, whether or not Syl and I go is unimportant, really.'

'You speak for yourself, Howard Lord!' retorted his wife sharply. 'I was looking forward to a night out. We don't get many, goodness knows. We don't have an in-house child-minder!'

'That'll do, Syl,' muttered Howard gruffly, flashing his sister an appealing look. 'The fact is,' he flushed, 'we wondered if the twins could stay here tonight, Mum. I know you've got company, but if Antonia shared with you, the twins could have her bed.'

It was ironic, thought Antonia later that evening, as she applied her mascara. She didn't even want to go to the theatre, and she suspected Reed didn't either. But because of Sylvia, and her complimentary tickets, they were going, and what was more, when they got back, Mrs Lord would be waiting for her daughter to share her bed.

She didn't wear the new dress. It seemed a shame to have to conceal it beneath the woollen coat her mother had lent her, and besides, they were eating at home before meeting Howard and Sylvia outside the theatre.

The twins were as naughty as usual, making Susie cry by hiding Garfield in the dirty clothes basket and driving Mrs Lord wild by chasing madly about the house. Eventually, it was Reed who settled them, threatening them both with corporal punishment if they didn't behave themselves while he and Antonia were out, and softening the blow by promising to take them home on Sunday morning in the Lamborghini, if they made no further nuisance of themselves.

'You'll make a remarkably good father one day,' said Antonia carelessly, as they drove away, and then could have bitten out her tongue at the obvious connotations of her pronouncement. She didn't want to think about Celia—not tonight—and she turned her head away to hide her pained expression.

'I hope so,' Reed answered behind her, as she struggled to get her emotions under control. 'My parents can't wait to have a grandchild. Someone like Susie would suit them very well.'

Antonia moistened her lips. 'I doubt if they'd agree with you,' she murmured, and she sensed his wry amusement.

'Well, I suppose they would prefer for me to be the father of my children,' he conceded softly. 'They'll leave the choice of the mother up to me.'

Antonia's fingers tightened round the slim purse in her lap. 'But it wouldn't do for you to produce a little bastard, would it?' she got out bitterly, and she felt the sudden intensity of his gaze.

'What is that supposed to mean?' he enquired, and her tongue circled her lips once again.

'Well,' she ventured tensely, 'accidents can happen.'

'What are you trying to say?' he exclaimed wearily, and all her pent-up frustrations burst from her like a flood.

'You don't care, do you?' she cried tremulously. 'Oh, I know it's unlikely that that particular stroke of lightning should strike twice in the same place, but it doesn't matter to you, does it?'

Reed brought the car to an abrupt halt and turned

towards her. 'Why are you doing this?' he demanded harshly. 'Why are you saying these things? Who are you trying to hurt? Me? Or yourself?'

Antonia was trembling violently, but when he would have put his hands upon her, she shook them off. 'I can't hurt you, can I?' she choked. 'You wouldn't allow that to happen.'

'Antonia, for Christ's sake!' Reed thrust long impatient fingers through his hair. 'We can't talk about this now!' He shook his head. 'What do you want me to say?'

'Nothing.' Antonia withdrew into her corner, putting as much distance between them as it was possible to achieve. 'Go on. We're going to be late. We don't want to keep Howard and Sylvia waiting.'

'I don't give a damn about Howard and Sylvia,' Reed told her roughly. 'Hell, why did we let them talk us into going to see this bloody play? I wanted to be alone with you—not obliged to make small-talk with your brother and his wife!'

Antonia bent her head. She could not doubt the sincerity of his words, and she knew a blind impatience with herself for precipitating such a scene. 'I'm sorry,' she said unhappily, as he swung back to the wheel, and with a muffled oath, he set the car in motion again.

'So am I,' he muttered harshly, his features set in grim lines, and for the remainder of the journey there was silence between them.

Antonia had even less reason for enjoying the evening when, after a couple of whiskies at the bar in the interval, Howard admitted that it had been Sylvia's idea to get the tickets. 'You mean—they weren't complimentary tickets?' Antonia demanded of her brother, as Reed discussed the first half of the play with Sylvia.

'Syl wanted an evening out,' said Howard placatingly, already realising he had said too much. 'And you know how our mother hates to come out to Tynemouth to baby-sit. It seemed the ideal solution. And you are enjoying the play, aren't you? I'm sure Reed is. He's a good chap. I like him.'

It was supposed to be an apology, but Antonia found it hard to forgive him. Still, she reflected, as she and Reed drove back to Gosforth, Howard was not to know how precious the time she spent with Reed was. And perhaps it was fate, after all, stepping in to prevent her from making another mistake.

The house was dark when they let themselves in, but Antonia guessed her mother would still be awake. Mrs Lord always liked to assure herself that all the occupants of the house were safely home and the doors securely locked before she went to sleep. And when Reed suppressed a yawn, Antonia realised she had selfishly forgotten how tired he must be.

'Do you want a drink?' she asked, adhering to the rules of politeness, but Reed only looked at her with guarded eyes.

'Not tonight,' he responded evenly, loosening his tie and unbuttoning his shirt. 'Would you think me very rude, if I went up to bed?'

It was late on Sunday afternoon when they finally left Newcastle. Susie was tearful, as usual, doubly so because the twins' presence had spoiled the morning for her, and she clung frantically to her mother when Antonia tried to get into the car.

'You're coming to London in two weeks,' Antonia consoled her gently, extricating the little girl's arms from around her neck. 'Less than that, actually, because Nanna's going to bring you down on Friday, and she says she'll stay until Tuesday, how about that?'

'Will Reed be there?' asked Susie innocently, and Antonia cast an awkward look at his dark face.

'We'll see,' she murmured uncomfortably, aware of her mother's eyes upon her, and Susie had to be content with the half-promise.

'Drive carefully,' called Mrs Lord, as the car began to move, and Reed lifted his hand in farewell as they turned out of the close.

To begin with, the traffic in the city took all of Reed's attention, and Antonia lay back in her seat, wondering what he was really thinking. A surreptitious glance at her watch advised her it was already four-thirty, and by her estimation it would be half-past nine or ten o'clock by the time they got back to London. Much too late to have dinner, she reflected, unless he stopped on the motorway. But looking at his grim face she suspected he was eager to reach his destination, and her heart ached at the knowledge that she had generated his mood.

The roads were not busy once they left the outskirts of Gateshead, and paying little attention to the speed limit, Reed's foot descended on the accelerator. The miles were eaten up at a steadily increasing rate, and she dare not disturb his sombre concentration. She was not afraid. Reed drove fast, but safely, and there was a certain exhilaration in passing every other vehicle on the road. Nevertheless, it shortened the journey considerably, and it was barely eight o'clock when Reed suddenly signalled his intentions to leave the M1, and turned instead on to the Aylesbury road.

Antonia, who had been anticipating their arrival at the flat with some apprehension, turned to look at him. 'Where are we going?'

'Stonor,' he said flatly, negotiating a pair of slow-moving vehicles and picking up his speed. 'As you're already prepared for the office, I thought we could spend the night there, and I'll drive you in to work in the morning.'

Antonia's heart fluttered. 'Spend the night at your house, you mean?'

'If you have no objections,' he conceded harshly, his fingers flexing tiredly against the wheel.

Antonia caught her breath. 'I—I thought you were mad at me,' she faltered.

'I am,' he agreed shortly, slowing for some traffic lights. 'But I'm also in love with you, and somehow I've got to convince you of that!'

By the time the Lamborghini turned between the gates of the gravelled drive that ran up to the house, Antonia had convinced herself she must have imagined

Reed's terse words. He could not have said he *loved* her, she told herself fiercely. She was tired, and so was he, and somewhere between his lips and her ears, an error had been made. It was probably her, she chided herself bitterly. She was confusing her feelings with his. Reed didn't love her; he loved Celia Lytton-Smythe. For her he felt a fleeting attraction; it was Celia who was to be his wife.

'I phoned on my way back from Tynemouth this morning,' Reed remarked briefly as Rose Macauley appeared at the door to greet them. Switching off the engine, he thrust open his door and got out, and Antonia was left to acknowledge that she could not have known. Reed had driven the twins home that morning, accompanied only by Susie. The sleek sports car was not built for two adults and three children, and besides, Antonia had not been invited.

'Sure, this is a surprise,' the little housekeeper observed, as Antonia slid out of the car. She smiled at Antonia and then turned her attention back to her employer, as she said: 'I've delayed the meal, just as you suggested, sir. But I'm sorry to have to say, Miss Patricia arrived late this afternoon.'

'Tricia!' Reed cast a rueful look in Antonia's direction, and then shook his head. 'Oh, well,' he remarked carelessly, 'I guess there'll be three of us for dinner, Rose. That doesn't create any problems does it?'

'Not to me,' replied Mrs Macauley meaningfully, and Reed's lean mouth curved into a smile.

'Nor to me, Rose,' he assured her drily, but Antonia's nerve fled at the prospect of meeting Reed's sister.

'Perhaps I ought not to stay,' she murmured, in a low voice, as they walked towards the entrance, and Reed looked down at her half-impatiently.

'I was polite to your brother, wasn't I?' he demanded, his hand in the small of her back compelling her forward. 'Now you can be nice to my sister, even if it is going to be an effort—for both of us!'

Patricia Gallagher met them in the hall. She, too, had

heard the car, it appeared, but her reactions were not as acute as Mrs Macauley's. 'Hi, Reed,' she ventured doubtfully, her grey eyes, so like her brother's, moving swiftly to the young woman beside him. 'I hope you don't mind me inviting myself for a couple of days. I didn't think you'd be here. Aren't you supposed to be in New York, or something?'

'I was,' drawled Reed, slipping his arm carelessly about Antonia's shoulders and drawing her closer to him. 'But—well, I got home sooner than I expected.'

'Yes.' Patricia's smile came and went, and Antonia realised the other girl was as nervous as she was. She was very like her brother: dark hair, grey eyes, a tall, slim body. But her features were much more feminine. The simple jersey tunic she was wearing bore the unmistakeable hallmark of good taste.

'You'll have gathered, this is my sister, Tricia,' Reed said now, resisting Antonia's efforts to break free of him. 'She always turns up at the least convenient moment.'

'And you must be—Mrs Sheldon,' Tricia declared, putting out her hand politely. 'I—Rose told me all about you.' She glanced awkwardly at her brother. 'I gather . . . I gather Celia's not with you.'

Shaking hands with his sister, Antonia knew her face was suffused with colour, but Reed was unperturbed. 'No, Cee's not with me,' he agreed, the look he cast in Antonia's direction turning her bones to water. 'And now, I suggest you let us freshen up before dinner. Which room are you occupying? Your usual one, I suppose.'

'Well, Rose did tell me that—Mrs Sheldon used that room the last time she was here,' said Tricia uncomfortably. 'But she said she didn't think you'd mind if—if your guest occupied the green room. You don't, do you?'

'We can live with it,' responded Reed drily, as Mrs Macauley came in carrying his overnight case and the small hold-all containing Antonia's suit and the dress he had bought her. 'I'll take those, Rose,' he added swiftly, releasing Antonia to take the bags from the housekeeper. 'We'll see you at dinner, infant. I'll show—my guest to her room.'

At the head of the staircase, Reed turned in the opposite direction from the one Antonia remembered. Instead, he escorted her to the fourth door along on the right, allowing her to open the door and precede him into the room.

Dropping his own case outside, he deposited her hold-all on the chest at the foot of the bed, and then retreated to the door. 'You know your way downstairs again, don't you?' he said, propping himself against the jamb. 'Don't be long. Rose will get impatient.'

'Reed—' As he would have left her, Antonia took a step towards him. 'Reed, I don't have anything to wear.'

'Wear the dress I bought you,' he muttered, his brooding gaze raking her slim figure in the simple shirt and jeans she had worn to travel in. 'You have brought it with you, haven't you?' And at her nod: 'I'll see you downstairs in twenty minutes.'

With the door closed behind him, Antonia drew a hasty breath. Twenty minutes seemed such a little time to come to terms with the situation, and her heart palpitated wildly at the prospect of what his sister must be thinking.

She paid little attention to her surroundings as she took a hasty shower in the perfectly matched bathroom. Like the other room, the misty greens and gold of the carpet were picked out in the covers and curtains, and the deliciously warm apartment banished the goose-pimples from her flesh.

Applying a little make-up, she remembered what Tricia had said about her room, and the realisation that the clothes she had seen in the closet there were Reed's sister's gave her an unwarranted lift. It was foolish, she knew, for if Celia did not occupy that room there was no doubt another room that she did. Or did she simply share Reed's apartments? Antonia mused unhappily. Although she had spent the weekend here, she still had no idea where the master of the house slept.

Dinner was served in the small dining room that

opened off the library. It was where she and Reed had had dinner the Saturday evening she had stayed at the house, and beforehand, they had drinks in the comfortable book-lined room adjoining.

'Did you go to New York with my brother, Mrs Sheldon?' Tricia asked, as the two girls sipped glasses of white wine seated on the leather sofa.

'No, she didn't,' Reed interposed briefly, from his position on the hearth. 'And I think you should call her Antonia, don't you?' His lips twisted. 'As our relationship is anything but formal.'

To Antonia's relief, Mrs Macauley's appearance to announce that dinner was served, saved the younger girl from making any response. With an eager: 'Thank goodness!' Tricia followed the housekeeper into the dining room, and Antonia met Reed's gaze with growing apprehension.

'You look beautiful,' he said, his hand at the nape of her neck preventing her from hastening after his sister. 'Just remember that.' His lips brushed her temple. 'Dinner will soon be over.'

She didn't know what he meant, and she was too unsure of herself to probe. Instead, when Rose Macauley appeared in the doorway again, evidently impatient for them to come and start their meal, Antonia took the opportunity to break away from him, and Tricia looked up diffidently as the other two took their places.

The food was as delectable as anything Mrs Braid had produced on Antonia's previous visit. A smoked salmon mousse was followed by a creamy vegetable soup; and medallions of veal, cooked in wine and served with tiny button mushrooms, were a forerunner to the raspberry meringues which completed the meal.

Antonia noticed that for all her slender figure, Tricia had a healthy appetite, whereas she found it incredibly difficult to eat anything. Reed, too, seemed to find the wine which accompanied the meal far more to his taste than his cook's culinary expertise, and Mrs Macauley clicked her tongue disapprovingly as she took their plates away.

'What do you do to him, Mrs Sheldon?' she exclaimed, as Reed's plate was returned to the kitchen virtually untouched. 'Sure, the man must be sick of something to be starving himself like this! Let's hope that by the morning, he'll have more appetite for his breakfast!'

Antonia's face burned, and even Reed gave the old woman an impatient glare. 'Your tongue's so sharp, it will cut your throat one of these days,' he essayed narrowly, as she served the coffee. 'As a matter of fact, we'll be leaving early in the morning, so you can forget the sarcasm.'

Rose grimaced and left them, and Tricia expelled her breath on a rueful sigh. 'She really is the limit!' she exclaimed, looking sympathetically at Antonia. 'You mustn't take any notice of her. She thinks she has the right to say what she likes!'

Antonia forced a faint smile, but she couldn't meet Reed's eyes, and a few moments later he pushed his chair back and got to his feet. 'Look, I think we should all get an early night,' he remarked heavily. 'I've promised to drive Antonia in to work in the morning, and as she starts at nine, we've got to leave here at seven o'clock at the latest.'

'And, of course, you'll still be jet-lagged,' said his sister, nodding. 'You're going to find it pretty difficult to open your eyes at seven o'clock.'

'I know that.' Reed regarded her levelly. 'So—good night then.'

'Good night.'

Tricia smiled up at him over the rim of her coffee cup, and because it would look too suspicious if she attempted to accompany him upstairs, Antonia echoed the younger girl's response.

'See you—see you in the morning,' she offered, trying to sound casual, and Reed inclined his head politely before leaving the room.

Left alone with Tricia, Antonia waited apprehensively for the words of censure she was sure the younger girl wanted to voice. But they never came. Instead, Reed's sister offered her more coffee, and when their cups were filled, she said quietly: 'I'm so pleased I've had this chance to meet you. You're different from what I expected.'

'Am I?' Antonia assumed Rose Macauley had been less than generous in her assessment. 'Well—I hope it's an improvement.'

'It is.' Tricia's lips twitched. 'I think we've all been labouring under a misapprehension.'

'All?' Antonia frowned. 'You mean—Rose; Mrs Macauley?'

'No, I mean my parents,' said Tricia evenly. 'I might as well be honest. It's no accident that I'm here, Antonia. When Reed phoned and said you would be spending the night here, Rose contacted my mother and she contacted me.'

CHAPTER ELEVEN

ANTONIA let herself into her room with an aching sense of weariness. The conversation she had had with Tricia had left her feeling troubled and confused, and although Reed's sister had said nothing to upset her, she was upset nevertheless.

It had been such a shattering discovery to make: that Mrs Macauley should have taken it upon herself to inform Reed's parents of their son's aberrations. She could imagine what the Gallaghers must be thinking. And the fact that she was a divorcee could only have added to their anxieties.

Not that Tricia had said anything of the sort. On the contrary, she had been amazingly casual about the whole affair. 'You must understand,' she had said swiftly, reacting to Antonia's shocked embarrassment at her words, 'we have always been a very—close family. And when Rose informed my mother that you and Reed had spent the weekend here, alone, Mummy was quite disturbed.'

'I'm sure she was.' Striving for composure, Antonia had shaken her head. 'Does she think I'm trying to break up Reed's engagement?'

'Well—she was concerned that Reed hadn't told her about you,' Tricia confessed. 'I mean—Celia wasn't Reed's first girlfriend, or anything like that, but he never used to bring his—well, Celia's the only one who's ever stayed at Stonor. Until now.'

Antonia's face was burning. 'I don't know what to say——'

'Don't say anything,' said Tricia ruefully. 'Reed's probably going to wring my neck for talking to you. But—oh, you know what mothers are. She just wanted to know what you were like.'

Antonia shook her head. 'She doesn't have to worry,

165

you know,' she murmured uncomfortably. 'Our ... relationship—mine and Reed's that is—it's not—important.'

'Don't you think so?' Tricia's eyes were suddenly very like her brother's. 'You know, I'm tempted to agree with Rose, harridan though she is. I've never known Reed lose his appetite before.'

Now, Antonia closed her door and leaned exhaustedly against the panels. What did it matter what Tricia thought, she asked herself, or Mrs Gallagher either? After this weekend, she was determined not to see Reed again. It was becoming too bittersweet, too painful; too deceptively easy to fool herself they were hurting no one. They *were* hurting people, themselves most of all—or so Tricia would have her believe, if her statement was true.

Straightening away from the door, she started to unzip her dress. It was late, and she was tired. The problem of how to cope with the situation would have to wait until the morning. Right now, she wanted to lose herself in oblivion, and forget that he'd ever said he loved her.

Stepping out of her dress, she turned, and as she did so, her breath caught in her throat. She had been so intent in her misery, she had scarcely noticed the fact that her bed was turned down and that someone was already reclining between the fine silk sheets. In the subdued lighting of the bedside lamp, Reed's lean face had a hollow vulnerability, the sooty fringe of his lashes resting on his cheeks. He was asleep, his brown body dark against the pastel green of the pillows.

After what she had been telling herself, she knew she should wake him and send him back to his own room, but she didn't. Consoling herself with the thought that Reed needed his sleep, she went into the bathroom and removed her make-up. Then, after cleaning her teeth, she took off her tights and her bra, and came back to the bed. She had brought no nightdress with her, as she had expected to be sleeping at the flat tonight, so she kept her slip on instead.

Folding back the covers, she slid carefully into the bed, trying not to disturb him, and then nearly jumped out of her skin when he said huskily: 'What a hell of a time you've been!'

'You're awake!'

The words were little more than a squeak, and he moved lazily nearer, his arm sliding beneath her head and pulling her towards him. 'Did you really think I wouldn't be?' he demanded, burying his face in the scented hollow between her breasts, and trembling a little, she felt his tongue against her skin.

'You shouldn't be here,' she protested, struggling to maintain a sense of reality. 'Reed, what would your sister think?'

'I don't give a damn what my sister thinks,' he retorted, his impatient fingers sliding beneath the hem of her slip. 'This is my house, and finding an unwanted visitor here, is no reason to spend another frustrated night.' He made a sound of aggravation. 'What on earth did you leave this on for? You're not cold, are you?'

Cold? Antonia drew an unsteady breath. Her body was as suffused with warmth as her face had been earlier, and the sensuous brush of his aroused body against her thighs was bringing a distinct ache to the pit of her stomach.

'Reed—your mother . . . that is, Mrs Macauley *told* your mother you and I had spent the weekend here,' she breathed, as the satin slip was cast aside, and she felt the delicious softness of the sheet against her bare back. 'Reed—are you listening to me?'

'Do you want me to?' he murmured, his mouth devouring hers with sensual abandon, and her senses swam beneath the moist invasion of his tongue.

'Reed——'

'All right. I guessed she might,' he responded carelessly, taking one full breast in his hand and loving the swollen nipple with hungry urgency. 'Oh, love, I don't care what Rose says, or what my mother says, or what anyone says, but you.' He slid lower, his hand finding the soft inner curve of her thigh. 'You are the only person I care about. God, don't you believe me?'

The drugging intimacy of his lips suspended all other thought. Her hands sliding possessively over the muscled curve of his hips, Antonia couldn't think of anything else but the immeasurable delight of his lovemaking, and Reed was not immune to the tentative sexuality of her caress. With a muffled groan, he moved over her, crushing her breasts beneath him, and the pulsating power of his manhood sought its silken sheath . . .

Reed dropped Antonia outside the institute at five minutes past nine the following morning. 'Sorry, you're late,' he remarked softly, as she made to get out, and Antonia cast him a tremulous glance before reaching for the door handle. 'I'll call you,' he said, his hand on her wrist delaying the moment, but Antonia shook her head.

'Don't,' she said huskily. 'I—I don't want us to see one another again!' and with this damning indictment, she scrambled out of the car.

He was tempted to go after her, but the prospect of trying to reason with her here deterred him. Besides, he had other things he wanted to do, other things he *had* to do, before seeing Antonia again, and with a smothered oath, he let her go, his lungs constricting in his chest.

Dear God, he thought incredulously, when had it hit him that what he felt for Antonia was more than just a desire to go to bed with her? Oh, he wanted that, of course. Just remembering the night they had just spent brought a disruptive stirring in his groin, but his feelings went far beyond the physical. Even when he was making love to her, even when their bodies were fused in the mindless aftermath of their mutual passion, he wanted to possess her mind, as well as her delectable form, and the emptiness he felt whenever he left her, would not easily be displaced.

He knew she was not indifferent to him. When she stopped fighting him, her hunger was as great as his, and he had never known a woman who so exactly matched his moods. There had been other women, lots of other women, ever since he had been old enough to attract the attention of the opposite sex. But, none of them, and most particularly, not Celia, had ever given him the satisfaction—both mentally and physically— that Antonia did. She was so delicious, so delightful, so lovable—so everything he wanted in a woman. It was funny—whenever he had anticipated his marriage to Celia, it had been in terms of their having a family, of giving his parents the grandchild they craved. With Antonia, whether or not they had a baby didn't come into it. He wanted her, he wanted to be with her, and he was selfish enough to enjoy the prospect of sharing her with no one but her daughter.

He reached Eaton Lodge in only a few minutes, and parking the Lamborghini on the forecourt, he thrust open his door and strode into the building. With a bit of luck, Celia would not have left yet for the shop, but if she had, he would just have to make other arrangements. He could always take her out to lunch, he reflected reluctantly, although he did not welcome the prospect of prolonging the agony. He wanted to make a clean break, and as decently as possible. He was not the kind of man to take any satisfaction in what he had to do, and if she wanted to tell their friends she had jilted him, he was quite prepared to go along with it. The way it was done didn't matter to him, just so long as he gained his freedom. How was it Shakespeare had put it, he mused wryly: *if it were done ... then 'twere well it were done quickly*. He grimaced, and as he made for the stairs, Mrs Francis called his name.

'Mr Gallagher,' she exclaimed. 'You're an early caller.'

Reed paused and turned. 'Good morning, Mrs Francis,' he responded resignedly. 'Yes. Is Miss Smythe still at home, do you know?'

'Miss Lytton-Smythe hasn't left to my knowledge,' the caretaker's wife declared knowingly. 'And I usually hear her go. And Miss Ashford, too.'

'I'm sure you do.' Reed turned back to the stairs, and then had another thought. 'Er . . . Liz, Miss Ashford, I mean; did you say she *had* left?'

'I think she's been away for the weekend,' confided Mrs Francis, with a frown. 'Yes. I believe she was spending the weekend in Leicestershire. With the— Stockwells. Would that be right?'

'You're very well informed, Mrs Francis,' Reed complimented her drily. 'Okay. Thanks. I'll just go up and see if Celia's ready to leave.'

He was conscious of her watching him round the curve of the stairs, and he pulled a wry face. He would be glad to get Antonia out of this place. He did not appreciate having to explain his intentions every time he entered the building.

He pulled his keys out of his pocket as he reached Celia's door, but having second thoughts, he pressed his finger on the bell. As he waited, he extricated her key from the others on his keyring and dropped it into his pocket. Celia could have it back again. He had no further use for it.

It seemed ages before she came, and he had rung the bell several more times before he heard the sound of the slip-chain being removed. It was just as well he hadn't tried to get in, he reflected. Evidently Celia was still locked up for the night. He shook his head. For once, he felt grateful to Mrs Francis. Without her intervention, he would probably have imagined Celia had already left.

The door opened slowly and Celia, a thin silk kimono pulled carelessly about her, peered out through narrowed lids. 'Reed!' she exclaimed faintly, identifying the lean dark individual propped indolently outside her door. 'Y—you're back!'

'As you see,' agreed Reed evenly, straightening from his lounging position. 'I got back on Friday, actually.'

'*Friday?*' Celia blinked, and if Reed had not been so concerned with his own problems, he would have taken more account of the faintly furtive glance she cast behind her.

'Friday,' he confirmed now, aware that their voices could carry down the stairs. 'Are you going to invite me in? I've got something to tell you, and I'd as soon say it in private, if you see what I mean.'

The meaningful look he sent down the stairs was self-evident, and Celia's tongue appeared to circle her parted lips. 'Well, I—you couldn't come back later, could you, darling?' she murmured awkwardly. 'You see—Liz hasn't been at all well. I've been up with her half the night. And I really am—absolutely exhausted!'

Reed could believe it. She looked pale and hollow-eyed, and if Mrs Francis had not been so sure about Liz spending the weekend with the Stockwells, Reed would never have doubted her. But there was a curious smell in the air, a sickly sweetness that Reed had smelt once before in his life, and because he could identify it, his cool grey eyes narrowed.

'Are you sure it's Liz who's been sick?' he enquired tensely, the connotations that immediately sprang to his mind causing him to speak with unnecessary violence. 'For Christ's sake, Cee, why didn't you tell me you were on that stuff!'

'What stuff?' asked Celia indignantly, trying desperately to refute his allegations, but Reed could only see his plans for the future—and Antonia—crumbling about him.

'You're crazy, do you know that?' he demanded savagely, pushing her inside and slamming shut the door with his foot. Thrusting her ahead of him into the living room, his jaw was tight with frustration. How could he tell her now, he was asking himself, when his own responsibility for what had happened had to be acknowledged?

'Reed, will you get out of here?' Celia's voice was rising shrilly with emotion, and he thought she could have no idea how much he wanted to do just that.

'When we've talked this through,' he declared, slamming his hands into his pockets. 'God—I thought you had more sense! Where the hell did you get the stuff?'

'Que se passe-t-il?'

The sound of a third voice brought Reed round with a start, his eyes widening disbelievingly at the sight of the thin dark man who had appeared from the direction of the bedrooms. Barefoot, hair tousled, the bathrobe pulled around him of evidently feminine design, he gazed across the room at them, aghast, and Celia rounded on him in angry protest.

'Raoul!' she exclaimed. *'Es pèce d'imbecile! Je t'ai dit de rester dans la chambre——'*

'I do speak French, Cee,' Reed put in drily, a faintly sardonic twist lifting the corners of his mouth. Hell, he thought, with rueful self-derision, no wonder Celia had been so reluctant for him to enter the apartment. With Liz Ashford away, how could she explain this?

'You don't understand, Reed,' Celia blurted in confusion, as she saw the dawning comprehension in his face. 'Darling, I only offered Raoul a bed for the night, because it was late when he brought me home. We'd been out to dinner. I thought you were away. You said you'd be away all weekend. Heavens, you don't imagine there's any more to it, do you? Honestly, Reed, would *I* do a thing like that?'

If Antonia had half-hoped that Reed might meet her from work that evening, she was disappointed. There was no sign of the Lamborghini as she emerged from the institute, and she told herself she was glad as she took her place at the bus stop.

There was no sign of the car at Eaton Lodge either, even though she had entertained the thought that he might be waiting for her there. And after all, he had to come and see Celia some time, she acknowledged unhappily. If she was going to carry on with her life in London, she had to accept that so long as Celia lived in the same building, their paths were bound to cross, sometimes.

She was making herself a sandwich when she heard someone knocking at her door, and her heart lifted wildly at the sound. It had to be Reed, she thought apprehensively. No one else was likely to call. And although she longed to see him, she determinedly ignored the summons.

'Mrs Sheldon! Antonia!'

The voice calling her name was definitely not Reed's, and Antonia expelled her breath. It was Celia. She was sure of it. And abandoning the makings of her sandwich, she mentally steeled herself before going to the door.

'Oh, you are in.' Celia's delicately moulded features drew into a relieved smile. 'I thought I wasn't mistaken. I followed you along Clifton Gate.'

'Did you?' Antonia controlled her colour with difficulty, the self-contempt she felt for deceiving the other girl causing her breath to catch in her throat. 'I'm sorry. I didn't see you.'

'No.' Celia glanced beyond her. 'Can I come in?'

Antonia hesitated, and then moved aside. 'If you like.'

Celia nodded, and stepped into the flat. 'Thanks. I won't keep you more than a few minutes.'

Antonia couldn't imagine what the other girl might have to say to her, and her heart palpitated erratically at the thought that Celia might have found out about her friendship with Reed. Friendship! Antonia's pulses raced. The passionate relationship they had shared bore little resemblance to that ineffectual description.

'Cosy,' remarked Celia now, looking round the flat with a faintly patronising air, and Antonia linked her fingers together.

'It suits me,' she said, biting back her indignation. 'I—what did you want to see me about? I have to phone my daughter in fifteen minutes.'

'Your daughter? Oh, yes, Reed told me about her,' remarked Celia carelessly, inspiring a sense of angry impotence in the woman she was addressing. 'She lives in the north of England with your mother, doesn't she? Reed seemed to think she was rather sweet.'

Antonia's features froze. 'He did?'

'Hmm.' Celia moved negligently across the floor, and

took up a position before the empty fireplace. 'You spent the weekend with him, didn't you? Oh, don't look so alarmed; I'm not about to scratch your eyes out, or anything silly like that. Reed told me all about it, and I've forgiven him. You don't imagine you're the first female to catch my fiancé's roving eye!'

Antonia's lips parted. 'I don't believe you . . .'

'No, they never do,' said Celia in a bored tone. 'Reed's girls, I mean. I suppose I can't blame them. They don't want to lose him. Reed really is awfully good in bed!'

Antonia took a deep breath and walked stiffly to the door. Pulling it open, she said tightly: 'I'd like you to leave, Miss Lytton-Smythe. Now. This minute. Or I might scratch your eyes out. That's an alternative you've not considered.'

Celia remained where she was for several seconds more, and then, as if not altogether trusting the gleam in Antonia's eyes, she sauntered back across the room. 'All right, all right,' she said. 'I'm going. But, honestly, my dear, to someone who's only thinking of your well-being, you are responding rather primitively.'

'Get out!'

'I will.' But Celia paused in the doorway nevertheless. 'As a matter of fact, there was another reason why I wanted to speak to you. I wanted to warn you, your lease on this flat won't be renewed at the end of June, as you anticipated. My father owns this building, as it happens, and although I shall be leaving myself in December—when I marry Reed—I refuse to feel your envious eyes spying on us every time we go in and out!'

Even five hours after Celia had left, Antonia was still trembling in the aftermath of what she had said. It had been horrible—*so horrible*—that Antonia knew she would never forget it. Hearing the other girl dismiss Reed's infidelities without turning a hair had been sick and humiliating. Yet, Celia was used to it; she had to be. It was the only explanation for the coolness with which she had spoken of his affairs. Antonia knew she ought to be feeling sorry for Celia, but she couldn't. If the girl was indifferent to Reed's unfaithfulness, then perhaps she had her own reasons for overlooking his transgressions.

Not that this conclusion made the situation any easier. Antonia had *loved* Reed; she loved him still, if she was honest with herself. Just because the object of her affections had not lived up to her expectations of him, did not automatically reduce her feelings. In every way, except one, he was still the only man she had ever truly cared about, and no matter what he did her love would survive. But it was painful. Even thinking about how he had deceived her made her want to throw up. She should never have come to London, she thought bitterly. This was her reward for abandoning her principles.

As yet, she hadn't given a lot of thought to Celia's pronouncement on the flat. She had no doubt that what the other girl had said was true, but she was too shocked, too numb, too *vulnerable* at present, to anticipate what she might do and where she might go. Those problems would have to wait until she was more equipped to deal with them. Right now, it was an effort to look beyond the next twenty-four-hours.

She was in her dressing gown, curled up on the sofa, trying not to remember where she had been at the same time the previous evening, when she heard the outer doorbell ring. It was well after eleven, and although she knew it could not be anyone for her, she slid off the couch and opened her door.

Mr Francis had done likewise, and she faced the elderly caretaker across the width of the hall. 'Someone must have forgotten their key,' he grunted, emerging from his doorway to reveal his hair-curlered wife behind him. 'I suppose I'd better answer it, but you never know at this time of night.'

'You be careful, Bert,' declared Mrs Francis, turning an anxious face in Antonia's direction, and because she felt obliged to do so, Antonia waited to ensure there was no trouble.

'Why—Mr Gallagher!' exclaimed the caretaker at

that moment, and Antonia turned horrified eyes on the door. It was Reed, brushing impatiently past the startled manager, his eyes on her shocked face as he strode unmistakably towards her.

Without giving herself time to have second thoughts, Antonia immediately stepped back inside her flat and closed the door. She had no intention of speaking to Reed tonight, particularly when he was evidently on his way to see Celia. Let the Francises think what they liked. She was not to blame if they thought she was rude.

She had scarcely slipped the safety chain into place before there was a hammering at the door. 'Antonia!' exclaimed Reed with evident impatience. 'What the hell are you doing? Open up! Come on—I want to speak with you.'

Antonia pressed her back against the panels, as if her weight could add anything to its security, and said steadily: 'Go away, Reed. What do you think you are doing? You have no right to embarrass me like this!'

'Embarrass *you*!' he echoed harshly. 'How do you think I feel, yelling at you through a door? Oh, for Christ's sake, let me in! Before Francis gets suspicious and calls the police!'

'He wouldn't do that.'

'Wouldn't he? Are you prepared to take that risk?' Reed expelled his breath wearily, his voice losing its aggression. 'Look, I've got to see you, Toni. Don't make me spell it out in front of witnesses.'

Pressing her lips together, Antonia tried to resist the insidious appeal of his voice, but she could not let him tell her lies in front of Mrs Francis. She still had to live here, for another couple of months, at least, and was it really a lesser evil to pretend this had not happened?

Taking a deep breath, she slipped the chain and opened the door. Immediately, Reed widened the space she had created to allow him to step inside, and with an ironic smile at Mrs Francis, still hovering doubtfully across the way, he firmly closed the door behind him.

CHAPTER TWELVE

BACKING away from him, Antonia put the length of the sofa between them before permitting herself to meet his eyes. But the intensity of their expression was hardly tempered by the distance, and she shifted a little nervously beneath the censure of his gaze.

'Would you mind telling me what all that was about?' he demanded quietly. 'I realise it's late, and I've probably got you out of bed, but it surely must have occurred to you that my being here must be important.'

Antonia shrugged, her eyes defensive. 'I—I assumed you'd come to see Celia,' she declared, hiding her shaking hands in her pockets. 'Isn't it a little foolhardy, coming here at this time of night, even for you?'

Reed put up a hand and pulled the knot of his tie away from the collar of his pale grey shirt. The tie was silk, like the shirt, Antonia noticed inconsequently, his suit several shades darker and, as usual, immaculately pressed.

'I suppose I deserve that,' he said, when his collar button was unfastened, and his hand through his hair had made it attractively dishevelled. 'I should have got here sooner, and I would have if the eight o'clock plane hadn't sprung a fault.'

Antonia blinked. 'The plane?' she echoed blankly. 'What plane?'

'The plane from Dublin,' replied Reed, glancing about him. 'Can I sit down? I really am pretty bushed!'

Antonia shook her head confusedly, and then made a hasty gesture of acquiescence. 'You've been to Dublin to see your parents,' she essayed carefully. 'To—explain about our weekend at Stonor.'

'In a manner of speaking,' said Reed wearily, subsiding on to the sofa and resting his head back against the cushions. 'I had to speak to my father. And my mother deserved an explanation.'

'Of course.' Antonia drew her hands out of her pockets and gripped the arm of the sofa. 'I assume they don't condone your profligacy. Or perhaps they do. I'm not very expert when it comes to judging people's characters!'

Reed regarded her blankly, and then he shook his head. 'What old-fashioned words you use,' he remarked, pushing himself up from his lounging position. 'Perhaps you'd tell me what you mean by that assessment. Do I take it you consider my character beyond redemption?'

Antonia shivered. 'I think we should stop playing games.'

'Oh, so do I.' Reed's face was broodingly intent.

'So?'

'So what?' Reed frowned. 'What particular game are we playing now? The same game you've been playing, ever since you realised there was something between us?'

'No.' Antonia flushed. 'There is—nothing between us. You know it, and I know it, so I think you should stop pretending there ever was.'

Reed blinked and then, deliberately, he got up from the sofa again. 'Okay,' he said. 'What's happened? Why are you acting like I was the prodigal son? I know what you said this morning, and I know why you said it, but that doesn't apply any more.' He bent his head, his cheeks hollowing as he sucked in his breath. 'Cee and I are through. We split up this morning. The reason why I went to Dublin was to tell my parents about *us*!'

Antonia's reaction was a disbelieving gasp, and she let go of the arm of the sofa to step further away from him. 'I—I—how can you say such things?' she got out incredulously. 'I spoke to Celia this afternoon, and she told me in no uncertain terms that you were *not* through at all.'

Reed's head jerked up. 'You spoke to Cee this afternoon?'

'I've just said so.' Antonia quivered. 'She told me all

about ... all about the relationship you have with her!
It was what I expected—what I deserved, I suppose—
but it really wasn't necessary. I had already decided
what I had to do.'

'Had you?' Reed's face was grim. 'And I suppose
that's what this little charade is all about! It's your—
futile way of demonstrating that you still have a choice
in the matter!'

'It's not futile——'

'Isn't it? *Isn't it?*'Without giving her a chance to
escape him, Reed obliterated the space between them,
grasping her wrists with brutal fingers and twisting her
arms behind his back. The action brought her up
against him, her shocked reaction coming too late to
save her. Using his superior strength, Reed ground his
hard mouth down on hers, and as she struggled to free
herself, she felt the taste of her own blood in her mouth.

She fought him then, but after that first bruising
assault, Reed's lips softened and gentled. With insistent
persuasion, his tongue coaxed her lips to part, and the
moist invasion that followed made a nonsense of her
efforts to resist him.

Sensing her confusion, Reed released her wrists to
permit his hands to slide possessively across her back,
and arching her body towards his, he allowed a
shuddering sigh to escape him. 'Dear God, don't you
know I love you?' he muttered, in a voice that was
amazingly unsteady. 'Why do you persist in believing
anyone else but me?'

Antonia trembled. 'Celia said——'

'Yes, I can guess what Celia said,' he cut in harshly,
'but she was lying.' His fingers slid into her hair and
holding her head between his palms, he added
emotively: 'Give me a little credit, will you? I was an
attractive financial proposition, if nothing else, and
Celia was always aware of it.'

Antonia looked up at him uncertainly. 'You're—
not—going to marry her?'

'Haven't I just said so?'

'I don't know.' Antonia could hardly take this in.

'Are you sure this isn't just another ploy to confuse me?'

'Confuse you?' Reed closed his eyes briefly, and then opened them again to reveal a nerve-shattering tenderness. 'Oh, *love*! If anyone's confused here, it's me!'

'But . . . but Celia——'

'Yes?' Reed inclined his head resignedly. 'Go on. You'd better tell me what Cee said, then I'll tell you what really happened.' He glanced behind him as he spoke, and with a determined expression, he sank down on to the sofa again, pulling her across his knees as he did so. 'But first——' and with devastating thoroughness his lips reduced her protests to a quivering submission. 'Go on,' he added, when her arms were about his neck, and she was weakly clinging to him. 'Before I lose all sense of this conversation.'

Antonia shook her head. 'You don't make it easy . . .'

'Nor do you,' he responded, toying with the cord of her dressing gown. 'Please: let's get it over with.'

Antonia moistened her lips, intensely conscious of the muscular strength of his thighs beneath hers. 'I . . . I . . . she came here at teatime, when I got home from work. She . . . she knew all about—Susie, and about the weekend we had spent together. She said you had told her.'

'I had,' agreed Reed laconically. 'Go on.'

Antonia swallowed. 'Why did you tell her?'

'Why do you think?'

'I don't know.'

Reed shrugged. 'Isn't it reasonable that I'd have to give the reasons why I was breaking our engagement?'

Antonia's lips parted. 'You've—really done that?'

Reed's mouth parted to accommodate hers. 'Do you doubt it?' he demanded, his breath almost suffocating her, and suddenly she didn't.

Almost incoherently she blurted out the rest of what Celia had said, glossing over the worst of her excesses, but leaving Reed in no doubt of his ex-fiancée's bitterness towards her. 'I . . . I suppose we had hurt her,' she finished at last. 'Poor Celia!'

'But you believed her,' he reminded her quietly, his fingertips stroking an invisible line from her shoulder to her waist, and Antonia bent her head.

'Yes,' she said, not excusing herself. 'I . . . I still can't believe that . . . that you could want me and not . . . not her.'

'Is that so?' Reed abandoned his line-drawing to cradle her cheek in his palm. Then, seeing the brilliance of unshed tears in her eyes, he added softly: 'I have to say, you don't deserve me.'

Antonia sniffed. 'Don't tease.'

'I'm not teasing,' he told her huskily. 'I'm just trying to make you see it's not important. All that unpleasantness with Cee, it doesn't mean a thing to us. And we have the rest of our lives to prove it.'

'Do you mean that?' Antonia touched his cheek, and he turned his lips against her palm.

'I'm not in the habit of making extravagant statements unless I mean them,' Reed assured her unevenly. 'And if you'd let me explain before jumping to conclusions, I'd have reassured you on that point.'

Antonia caught her lower lip between her teeth. 'I'm sorry.'

'And will you believe me if I tell you I'm not in the habit of lying—to anyone,' he appended drily. 'Nor did I give Cee any reason for jealousy until you came on the scene.'

'But why me?'

'Do you think I haven't asked myself that question?' Reed demanded ruefully, nuzzling her nape. 'My life was so carefully mapped out. There was never any question but that I would take over my father's position in the company, and Celia seemed a suitable addition to my status. I was fond of her, and we seemed compatible enough. It was only when I met you, I started questioning my complacency.'

'A most—unsuitable complication,' put in Antonia softly, and his hand ran possessively down her throat.

'Well, I will admit I fought it,' he muttered roughly. 'My feelings for you were anything but complacent, and

I didn't want the aggravation. Unfortunately, I didn't have much choice in the matter.'

Antonia hesitated. 'Are you sure?'

'Am I sure of what?' He turned her face towards him. 'Am I sure of what I'm doing? Oh, yes.' His mouth brushed hers and then he drew back to look into her face. 'Or do you mean, am I sure I love you?'

Antonia drew a trembling breath. 'Are you?'

'Let me put it this way,' he murmured, his tongue tracing the delicate contours of her ear, 'I don't know what you've done to me, but I can't contemplate my life without you. Does that answer your question?'

'Oh, Reed——'

She tightened her arms around his neck, and she felt his instant response to the lissom provocation of her yielding body. 'Oh, God, I want you,' he groaned, sliding the dressing gown off her shoulders and uttering a frustrated sound at the enveloping folds of her nightshirt beneath. 'Why do you always wear so many clothes!'

'I didn't know I'd be sleeping with you, did I?' Antonia responded huskily, assisting his removal of the offending nightgown, and Reed gave a sigh of approval when she was naked in his arms.

'Help me!' he said, shrugging off his jacket and tugging off his tie, and her fingers moved obediently to the buttons of his shirt.

But when he gathered her warm body against his, he didn't carry her into the bedroom as she had anticipated. 'I want you here—and now,' he told her thickly, wrapping his lean flanks about her, and Antonia discovered there was something rather erotic about making love on a sofa...

It was weeks later before Reed told her all of what had occurred the morning he visited Celia's apartment. And by then, he and Antonia were married, and spending their honeymoon on the exotic island of Tahiti in the south Pacific.

Everything had happened so quickly, sometimes

Antonia had to pinch herself to ensure she wasn't dreaming. But she wasn't. It was all marvellously real, and since the night Reed had talked his way into her flat, they had never been apart. She had moved out of the flat and into Reed's apartment the day after he had visited his parents in Ireland, and although she continued working at the institute until they were married, they had spent every free moment together.

The weeks before their wedding had flown. Antonia had had a long telephone conversation with her mother as soon as she was settled in the St James's Street apartment, and Mrs Lord had adopted a very knowing tone when she heard her daughter's news. But it had been Susie—and Reed's parents—who presented the biggest obstacle, and Antonia had not looked forward to her first visit to his family's home in County Wicklow.

And at first, there had been a certain restraint on the part of Reed's mother and father. It was to be expected, Antonia told herself, knowing she was marrying into a staunchly Catholic family, to whom her divorce from Simon made a church wedding out of the question.

But somehow, she didn't quite know how, the visit had not proved to be the disaster she had anticipated. Maybe, as Reed had intimated, when he came to her room that night, his parents could see that she was making *him* happy, and in the days that followed, Antonia had come to accept his assessment of the situation.

It was Tricia who eventually told her that it was much more simple even than that. 'They like you,' she said, pulling a wry face at her brother. 'They were always a little doubtful about Celia. She was never quite relaxed when she came to stay in the country.'

Susie's reactions had been reassuringly uncomplicated. She already liked Reed, and the knowledge that when her mother married again they would have a proper home life once more was a very persuasive factor.

'Will we live in the country?' she asked Reed, the first

weekend they took her and Antonia's mother to Stonor, and he had smiled.

'Would you like to?' he asked, and at her nod, he continued: 'Then, we'll have to see about finding you a pony, so that you can get about more easily,' and her whoop of delight had made her mother shake her head.

'Bribery and corruption,' she had teased Reed, and he had waited until later to exact a sweet punishment.

Waking on the morning of their last day in Tahiti, Antonia lay for several minutes without stirring, just looking at the man who had made her world so complete. It hardly seemed possible it was less than four months since they had first met. Now, she couldn't remember a time when he had not been an integral part of her life.

'What are you thinking?'

Reed's eyes had opened as she lay musing, and Antonia snuggled nearer to deposit a lingering kiss at the corner of his mouth. 'I was thinking how much I love you,' she admitted, shifting so that his possessive arm could close about her. 'I wish we never had to leave here.'

Reed's eyes were openly caressing. 'I thought you might be eager to get back home. That you might be missing Susie.'

Antonia sighed. 'Well, I do miss her, of course, but I know she's happy.' She ran her hand across his chest, loving the fine whorls of hair that curled confidingly about her finger. 'Your parents have been absolutely marvellous. Letting her stay with them.'

'Well, she seemed to take to them,' remarked Reed modestly, and Antonia's lips tilted.

'They spoil her,' she declared, remembering Susie's excited voice, the last time they had spoken to her on the phone. 'A pony *and* a dog of her own. She's never going to want to leave Drumbarra.'

'I think that's their idea,' said Reed, allowing a lazy laugh to escape him. 'Still, at least that takes the onus from us. They've got the granddaughter they always wanted.'

Antonia nodded, wondering how to phrase her next words. 'But would you mind?' she ventured carefully, watching his expression, 'if we added to our family rather sooner than you expected?'

Reed levered himself up on one elbow to look down at her. 'You're pregnant.'

'Hmm.'

'God!' He bent his head to give her a very disruptive kiss. 'How long have you known?'

'Since about the first week we were here,' admitted Antonia reluctantly, and his eyes widened incredulously.

'So why didn't you tell me?'

'I didn't want to—spoil our honeymoon.'

'How could that spoil anything?' demanded Reed huskily, his eyes running possessively down her body. 'Hell, we've been here four weeks, and you've known all that time!'

Antonia ran her fingers along the roughened curve of his cheek. 'Well, not definitely,' she murmured, colouring. 'These things take time.'

Reed shook his head. 'Do you mind?'

'Do you?'

'That's a crazy question,' he muttered huskily. 'Of course I don't mind! Just so long as you don't shut me out.'

Antonia moistened her lips. 'I—Simon was never interested' she confessed, by way of an explanation. 'When I told him I was going to have Susie, he asked if I wanted to get rid of it.'

'I'm not Simon,' said Reed forcefully, brushing back the silky hair from her temple with caressing fingers. Since their wedding, Antonia had allowed her hair to grow, and now it tumbled softly down her back. 'And— as it happens—I have something to tell you, too.'

'You do?' Antonia was apprehensive. Her eyes darkened. 'What is it?'

As if sensing her uncertainty, Reed lowered his length beside her and gathered her closer to him. 'Don't look so worried,' he told her softly, as anxious anticipation feathered along her spine. He brushed her lips with his thumb. 'I heard from my father a week ago, as you know. But I didn't tell you everything he wrote.'

Antonia's tongue circled her lips. 'It's not—Susie, is it?'

'No.' Reed was very definite on that point. He paused. 'Do you remember, we tried to contact Sheldon to organise the adoption order?'

'Yes.' Antonia held her breath.

'Well—I didn't want to tell you sooner, but Toni— *love*; Sheldon was drowned in the South China sea more than six months ago.'

'I think we should have a second honeymoon,' declared Reed, coming into the bedroom at Stonor with a towel draped carelessly about his hips. 'What do you think? Would you let Maria and my mother take care of our son as well as our daughter?'

Antonia, who was seated before the vanity unit in the master bedroom, rhythmically brushing her hair, lifted her slim shoulders. 'I thought you had that deal with the Canadians to attend to,' she reminded him. 'Didn't you tell me Cohen and the others were coming to dinner on Tuesday?'

'Well, yes, I did.' Reed came behind her, running possessive fingers under the thin straps of her slip and sliding them off her shoulders. 'But I've learned to delegate,' he added drily, bending to stroke sensuous lips across her soft skin. 'Wouldn't you like to spend a couple of weeks in the south of France? It's marvellous there at this time of the year.'

Antonia lifted her shoulder to facilitate his caress, and shivered in pleasurable anticipation. 'Reed, the Turners will be here in fifteen minutes,' she protested, when his questing hands slid beneath the lacy bodice to find the swelling fullness of her breasts, and he tossed the towel aside before drawing her up into his arms.

'They can wait,' he told her huskily, pressing the slip down over her hips. 'You did say Miss Forrester had taken the children to bed, didn't you?'

'I did say that, yes,' Antonia conceded laughingly, winding her arms around his neck. 'Oh, Reed, can we really take another two weeks to ourselves? Won't your parents think I'm a very indifferent mother?'

'My mother will be overjoyed to have charge of our family once again,' her husband assured her firmly, drawing her gently, but insistently towards their enormous four-poster. 'We went along with her wishes and had a second wedding in the church at Drumbarra. How could she deny us a second honeymoon?'

Antonia sighed reminiscently. 'It was a lovely wedding, wasn't it?' she murmured, remembering the tiny church at Drumbarra; the white surplices of the choirboys; the fragrant perfume of the flowers. 'I didn't think when you sent me that gorgeous bouquet last year that this year the same flowers would remind me of our wedding.'

'You did get them then,' remarked Reed drily, pulling her down on to the bed beside him and crushing her slender form beneath the muscular weight of his body. 'You never told me.'

Didn't I?' Antonia's slim fingers entwined in the hair at his nape. 'No—well, I didn't want to encourage you, did I?'

'That's the truth,' murmured her husband ruefully. 'Be thankful I didn't take no for an answer!'

'Oh, I'm very thankful for that,' responded Antonia fervently, and then gave herself up to the blissful possession of his mouth . . .

Here's how to get this special offer from Harlequin! As simple as 1…2…3!

AUGUST
TREASURY EDITION
COUPON

1. Each month, save one Treasury Edition coupon from your favorite Romance or Presents novel.
2. In four months you'll have saved four Treasury Edition coupons (<u>only one coupon</u> per month allowed).
3. Then all you have to do is fill out and return the order form provided, along with the four Treasury Edition coupons required and $1.00 for postage and handling.

Mail to: Harlequin Reader Service

RT1-A-2

In the U.S.A.
P.O. Box 52040
Phoenix, AZ 85072-2040

In Canada
P.O. Box 2800, Postal Station A
5170 Yonge Street
Willowdale, Ont. M2N 6J3

Please send me my FREE copy of the Janet Dailey Treasury Edition. I have enclosed the four Treasury Edition coupons required and $1.00 for postage and handling along with this order form.

(Please Print)

NAME_____

ADDRESS_____

CITY_____

STATE/PROV._____ ZIP/POSTAL CODE_____

SIGNATURE_____

This offer is limited to one order per household.

SUPPLIES LIMITED

This special Janet Dailey offer expires January 1986.

You're invited to accept 4 books and a surprise gift Free!

Acceptance Card

Mail to: **Harlequin Reader Service®**

In the U.S.
2504 West Southern Ave.
Tempe, AZ 85282

In Canada
P.O. Box 2800, Postal Station A
5170 Yonge Street
Willowdale, Ontario M2N 6J3

YES! Please send me 4 free Harlequin Presents® novels and my free surprise gift. Then send me 8 brand new novels every month as they come off the presses. Bill me at the low price of $1.75 each ($1.95 in Canada) — an 11% saving off the retail price. There are no shipping, handling or other hidden costs. There is no minimum number of books I must purchase. I can always return a shipment and cancel at any time. Even if I never buy another book from Harlequin, the 4 free novels and the surprise gift are mine to keep forever.

108 BPP-BPGE

Name _____ (PLEASE PRINT)

Address _____ Apt. No. _____

City _____ State/Prov. _____ Zip/Postal Code _____

This offer is limited to one order per household and not valid to present subscribers. Price is subject to change.

ACP-SUB-1